# COLD, LONE AND STILL

# COLD, LONE AND STILL

*Gladys Mitchell*

Michael Joseph
LONDON

First Published in Great Britain by Michael Joseph Ltd
44 Bedford Square, London WC1B 3DP
August 1983
Second Impression October 1985

ISBN 0 7181 2264 X

Composition by Allset, London
Printed in Great Britain by Hollen Street Press, Slough,
and bound by Hunter & Foulis Ltd, Edinburgh

To

The Companions of Margaret Hallahan

*with love from the author*

# CONTENTS

# *Prologue*

A week before I married Jane and moved with her into the house I had bought, I was sorting out the last odds and ends in my bachelor flat when I came upon some poems which I must have written to Hera in the early days of our love affair. One of them was only a rough draft, but I do not think I would have altered it much before I sent her a copy. I wonder whether she has kept it? I must have been head over heels in love with her at the time, or I would never have committed myself to praising her in verse.

As I read the poems, two thoughts came into my mind. One was the memory of a quotation from an early novel by Aldous Huxley in which he causes a young writer to say, 'Ah, what genius I had then!' The other was that I had better tear up the poems. It would never do for dear little freckled Jane to come across them after we were married. She would know that those passionate evocations could never, in this world or the next, apply to her. I suppose I should have known better than to submit to Hera's rulings about our conduct towards one another on the tour, but I was so besotted with her at the time that I suppose I would have agreed to anything she suggested. I was foolishly, fatally in error. As John Gay has said so rightly:

> 'Youth's the season made for joys;
> Love is then our duty.
> She alone who that employs
> Well deserves her beauty.'

Perhaps Hera did employ it while we were in Scotland, but, if she did, it was with Todd, not with me. She denied that she had done more than hold conversations with him, but I have never believed her. What man, finding a ripe peach nestling in the palm of his hand, would hesitate to gather it? From what I know of him, Todd would have had no scruples, and who shall blame him? Certainly not I.

He may have been an opportunist; I was undoubtedly a fool. The prayer book appears to make no distinction between the sins of commission and those of omission, so, in our different ways, I suppose Todd and I are equally guilty. Anyhow, Nemesis, with whom there is no arguing, has caught up with both of us, although I suppose most people would say that I am luckier than I deserve to be.

# 1

# A Test of Compatibility

Looking back, I think the preparations and the anticipation were by far the best part of the holiday. It was fun to assemble and check the gear, receive confirmation of the bookings and read and re-read the maps and brochures. The shopping was fun, too. We bought nailed boots, new anoraks and sweaters, ash-plants, a compass, electric torches, whistles in case we needed rescuing, a first-aid kit, and the latest make in rucksacks, framed to give the maximum comfort on the march. I mentioned emergency rations, but Hera said that we could stock up nearer the start of the walk.

According to the brochure, the trail could be walked in a week, but we decided upon a fortnight to allow for detours to any places of interest and also to give us time for stop-overs if the weather turned very wet, for even in June it was not to be trusted where we were going.

The walking tour was Hera's idea, not mine. We had talked over the possibility of living together before we were married, so that we could test our compatibility and all that sort of thing, but she said that it would be 'a something and a nothing, Comrie. We would know that it was only an experiment and not meant to last long, and we should be on our best behaviour all the time and that wouldn't be any test at all.' She went on to point out that a walking tour in hilly and often lonely country, with mishaps occurring daily, weary legs, blistered feet, rain, wind, mist and losing our way, would be the best means of discovering whether a partnership for life would be a viable proposition. 'If we can get through a fortnight like that without disaster, we can get through the next forty years,' she said.

'But supposing the weather stays fine, our boots fit, the scenery is as superb as the brochure promises, the hotels and youth hostels are first-rate and we don't meet with any mishaps at all?' I said. She laughed.

'If heaven smiled to *that* extent,' she retorted, 'I would ditch our engagement and hand you back the ring as soon as the journey ended.'

'But why?'

'Call it superstition or anything else you please, but that would be my reaction. Luck of that magnitude comes only from the Devil.'

I need not have worried. We were in for trouble all right, although not of any kind which I could ever have expected or foreseen.

Only over one thing did I get my way at the beginning of the trip. I was determined that it should kick off in comfort, so I had booked us in for the first night at the airport hotel near Glasgow. We did not get to it by air, of course, but I guessed that, however luxurious the place turned out to be, travellers would not be expected to dress for dinner. Indoor shoes, however, we did carry with us, nailed boots being regarded askance when worn on the polished or carpeted floors of the youth hostels and hotels in which we were to spend our nights.

I had booked separate rooms under our separate names at the airport hotel, and we met in the bar for cocktails at a quarter to seven. The train journey from London had been a long one and it was good to find that every bedroom had its bathroom and that the hot water was unlimited.

'I'm not sure this makes the most sensible start for the kind of holiday we've planned, but I must say it's very pleasant,' said Hera. She had changed her trousers and sweater for a rather slinky little frock and (not for the first time) I regretted the single rooms and a bed to which I knew I should not be admitted.

In the bar we made brief and inauspicious acquaintance with a man of whom we were to see more later. He stumbled as he passed us on his way from the bar to a small table and spilt some of his drink, for it was a glass of sherry and, as is the idiotic habit of bartenders, whether men or maids, it was full to the very brim, instead, after measurement, of being tipped into a larger glass, as I always request. Luckily, only the merest drop fell on to Hera's arm and that was bare, so no harm was done and my handkerchief soon did its job of mopping up. The fellow, a tall, rather good-looking chap, apologised and wanted to buy our drinks for us, but when I had refused this offer, Hera added, looking sweetly at him, 'Please don't bother. Some people can't help having two left feet.'

'I say, that was a bit strong, wasn't it?' I asked, when we reached our own little table.

'What was?'

'That crack of yours about two left feet. He apologised, and he didn't trip up on purpose.'

'That's where the two left feet came in. Don't be silly, Comrie. He was determined to speak to me.'

'But why? It wasn't as though you were here on your own.'

'I don't know why. He was on the train, you know.'

'Well, so were lots of other people.'

'He tried to get into conversation with me in the corridor. Oh, never mind him. Finish your drink. I'm starving.'

The dinner was a good one and I wished I had booked the hotel for at least one more night, but we were due to spend the next night at the youth hostel in the centre of the city. However, we had breakfast and lunch at the hotel and then took a bus. We had not enough luggage to warrant a taxi.

The youth hostel came under the Grade 1 category. It was open all the year round, had one hundred and twenty beds, was on the telephone and had a members' kitchen where hostellers could cook their own food. It also provided food for those who did not want to do their own cooking. It comprised two very large three-storey houses with a flight of steps up to the front door and was in a quiet street only a few minutes' walk from the bus stop.

Although we had been told that the peak months at the hostel were July and August, even in early June the place was pretty

full. We had not been in the common-room half an hour when
we were faced with the prospect of being urged to join the largest
party present. A fellow of about my own age approached us and
asked whether we were going along The Way.

'I'm afraid we haven't any religious convictions,' I said.

He laughed in the hearty, unconvincing way these muscling-in
types affect and said, 'Nothing like that, old boy, old boy! I
meant, are you doing the footslog to Fort William — the West
Highland Way, you know?'

'Heavens, no!' said Hera, before I could answer. 'We are merely
butterflying hither and yon.'

'Oh, what a pity! I'm trying to rope everybody in who is
doing The Way. Much jollier in a big party and we can all get together in the evenings and make whoopee, what!'

He seemed to have begun as he meant to go on, for, when we
came in, he had been chaffing other hostellers (among whom I
recognised our acquaintance of the cocktail bar) and shouting
with mirth at his own witticisms. A fellow to be avoided at all
costs, I thought.

'Sorry. We are only doing bits of this and that. We are not
seasoned walkers,' I said, 'and we have to respect our limitations.'

'Oh, well, anyway, come and meet the gang. There are eleven
of us, all told. Not bad, eh, considering I set out on my tod? But
I always reckon to pick up a mate or two at the hostels who will
be going my way. After all, it's a case of fellow-travellers, isn't
it? And I don't mean the nasty political kind. No, no. The more
the merrier, that's what I always say.'

'Eleven of you?' said Hera. 'A good thing we can't join you,
then, isn't it?'

'How come, fair one?'

'Because it would make the number up to thirteen and you
wouldn't want that, I'm sure.'

'Oh, I don't go for that sort of bunk. Come and get matey,
do.'

We could not get out of it without being boorish, although a
certain restlessness in the atmosphere indicated that some of the
company were not too happy, any more than we were, at being

roped in by this hot-gospeller of togetherness. He introduced himself as Neville Carbridge, but invited us to call him Nel. 'Only one "l", of course, old boy, old boy!' The only lone wolf was the fellow who had approached Hera on the train and then slopped drink on her at the airport hotel. I could see that Hera was not overjoyed at meeting him again. He was introduced to us as Barney Todd.

'Not Sweeney?' asked Hera, with the innocence she always displays when she looses off a barbed shaft.

'Now, now, fair one!' shouted the idiotic Carbridge. 'I thought of it first! You're not the only joker in the pack. Besides, I doubled up. I said, "Sweeney" and then I said, "I'm on my tod, too, so why don't we mingle, eh, old boy, old boy?" And now he's going to be the life and soul of the party, just like hot toddy! I say, I say! That's a good one, boys and girls! That's a *jolly* good one. See? Todd, toddy. Damme, I go from strength to strength, dashed if I don't. There's no holding me when I'm in the mood. Mind you, Todd is one of his aliases. He's got hot Spanish blood in his veins.'

One or two of the girls giggled, but I noticed that Todd himself was not amused. Personally I wondered whether I could restrain myself from assaulting Carbridge if he called Hera 'fair one' just once more. There was no stopping him on the subject of Todd, however. He put his hands to his forehead in the shape of horns and curvetted about, shouting, 'My name is Toro! Bring on the matadors! Toro! Toro! Bring on the toddy, for the toro, *el toro grande! Olé! Olé!*'

Todd took it calmly, but I don't think he liked being the butt of Carbridge's joking, or listening to the giggles of the girls. Apart from Carbridge and Todd, there were four other men. One, called James Minch, was accompanied by his sister Jane. Another rather cluttered-up chap seemed to be acting as bear-leader to four students, two men called Lucius Trickett and Freddie Brown, and two girls. Their leader's name was Andrew Perth, and it seemed to me that already he had the harassed look of a schoolmaster in charge of a pack of unruly children on a school outing.

It turned out that the students were from a London poly-technic and were 'doing' The Way as part of a course in geology. Perth had been hired by the college as an experienced guide who had a detailed knowledge of the countryside through which the walk would take his party, so that accounted for his being with the four youngsters and looking somewhat disconsolate.

The girls were called Coral Platt and Patsy Carlow. There were two other women, but these had come on their own and got themselves collected by Carbridge. I put them down as office girls, possibly minor civil servants. They turned out to be clerks in two different insurance firms. They had been friends from schooldays and always managed to fix their holidays for the same three weeks of the year. I spotted them eyeing the men in the party, particularly Todd, James Minch and myself.

James Minch was a straw-haired lad in, I guessed, his early twenties. It transpired that he had been president of his students' union and I could well envisage him in the part, for he turned out to have the gift of oratory to an extent which almost re-duced the exuberant Carbridge to silence, and during the course of the evening he gave us not only what I thought was a highly coloured and would-be humorous account of his college career, but also a description of his journey that day with his sister from their home town to the youth hostel in which, the prisoners of Carbridge, we were now stuck until the morning.

Jane Minch, the sister, was a redhead and her otherwise un-remarkable but pleasant young countenance was completely smothered in freckles. The office girls, Rhoda and Tansy (I did not get their surnames at the time), were a good deal older than any of the other women except Hera. They must have been going on for thirty. They were homely-looking girls, quite un-exciting, but probably kind-hearted. I thought that the men would write them off.

'I hope they have that much going for them, anyway. I mean, kind hearts,' I said to Hera next morning. 'They don't seem to have much else to recommend them.'

'They're all right,' said Hera, who was not always a defender of her sex. 'Isn't it about time we set out?'

I had delayed our departure deliberately in order to give the others a good long start. There had been some debate among them about whether to take the public transport to get to Milngavie, where The Way kicked off, or whether to footslog it, but this meant pavement-bashing and also it would add another seven miles or so to the long walk to Fort William. In the end it was decided, for the sake of the girls, that the public transport was to be favoured and, as we were going to use it too, although for a longer distance than theirs, I decided to let them get away first. I hoped we should never see them again. It was no part of our experiment to travel in convoy, even if we had liked the gang. The essence of our arrangement was that Hera and I should be on our own for a fortnight except for contact with hotel staff, hostel wardens and the cottagers who were to lodge us for an occasional night.

Hera had demurred when I insisted upon delaying our start, but I held on firmly and said, 'We've got to let that lot get clear away. Besides, I'd like to see as much as I can of the city before we leave. We'll have lunch somewhere and get on our way this afternoon. We're in no hurry. Don't you want to see the sights while we're here? We can still clock into the hotel at Drymen in plenty of time for a bath and dinner. How I hope we've seen the last of that laughing jackass and his party! My bet is that most of them will jettison him the first chance they get. Tomorrow morning we'll begin our tramping. We can start out directly after breakfast and take it easy to Balmaha. They will be a long way behind us by then, because we're getting transport to Drymen and they're walking all the way from Milngavie.'

There was plenty to see and do in Glasgow and, although we by no means covered everything, we did look around the twelfth-century cathedral, the museums, the art gallery, the shops in Sauchiehall Street, and we had lunch at one of the hotels. Hera was still slightly peevish and said that she could see no reason for my having delayed our start, but added that she had enjoyed her lunch. By mid-afternoon I felt we had had enough of sight-seeing and I could see that Hera was almost exhausted, so I suggested a slight change of plan.

'We're staying here for the night,' I said. 'We'll have some tea and then I'll book us in at the hotel where we had lunch.'

'Nonsense!' said Hera. 'We're booked in at Drymen and that's where we're going to spend the night.'

We had had a toss-up about the late start, so I did not argue. We went to Drymen, just as we had arranged to do, and turned in early. On the following morning we took a look around the little place before going on to Balmaha, where we had booked accommodation in a cottage.

Drymen is built around what, in England, would be called the village green. The hotel was excellent, the welcome cordial and the food good. We had been told that the shops were the best we should find for the next sixty miles, so we took the opportunity next morning to stock up on our rations and buy a couple more batteries for the torches. I also went to the bank, having previously arranged for this. I never like being short of ready cash, particularly on holiday when one never knows what unexpected calls may be made upon one's pocket.

'I wish we hadn't missed the earlier part of The Way,' said Hera. This, I thought, was rather unreasonable of her. We had agreed from the beginning to set out on our walk from Drymen. I began to wonder whether our relationship was going to stand the strain of a fortnight of pointless argument.

'If we had set out from Milngavie, we should have had the pleasure of Carbridge's company,' I pointed out. 'Be thankful we made the plans we did.'

'It's easy walking from Carbeth. I wasn't thinking of starting from Milngavie. From Carbeth, The Way goes through farmland and I don't suppose we shall see much of that further along the route, shall we?' she said.

I answered impatiently, 'Well, there is some between here and Balmaha.'

'We could have followed the old railway track,' she said. 'That would have been rather fun. Still, as you say, it's too late to think about that now, or the woods and the hills and the little river and the plank bridge and all the rest that's in the brochure.'

'You'll have all you want of hills and woods later on,' I told her.

To reach Balmaha we needed to cover only six and a half miles, so we lunched as early as we could at the hotel in Drymen and then made it an afternoon stroll. We identified Conic Hill and had to use a bit of the main road, but even then the journey was far from dull and we soon struck the countryside again as we turned past a farm. After that it was all farmland and forest and then on to grassland which merged into moorland. Hera was satisfied and there were no more complaints.

Some of The Way was rough, but the Garadhban Forest was worth any amount of rough walking. We climbed through sparse plantations of conifers and, looking back, we saw a great hill appearing over the top of the moorland ridge. We were sheltered to some extent in the forest itself, but when we came out to the moors again the air was fresh and the wind quite keen.

One of the strange things about hills and mountains is that they seem always to be shifting about as one travels. We had already seen Conic Hill when it appeared to be slightly behind us, but now we met it. As the day was fine, we could have taken the easier lower path, but Hera was determined to climb the hill for the sake of the view from the top, so she had her way without any dissent from me. I wanted no more arguments.

The bracken, as we climbed, was already high, but we managed to find the markers which charted The Way and, in any case, I had a map. The views from the top were magnificent, not the least being a panorama of Loch Lomond and its mountains.

Balmaha proved to be a tiny place. It had a shop where food could be bought, but already we had stocked up all we wanted to carry, so we found our cottage and introduced ourselves to our hostess. She had taken it for granted that we were married for I had booked for the two of us only in my own name, but Hera soon straightened matters out and I was despatched to a neighbour's cottage for the night and saw no more of my strong-minded fiancée until breakfast-time.

# 2
## *The Way Continues*

From Balmaha, The Way followed the east side of Loch Lomond. We had half thought of taking a boat-trip to the island of Inch-cailloch, the largest of the little archipelago at that end of the loch, but the brochure had mentioned the geology of the island as one of its attractions and, after our meeting with Perth and the polytechnic students, the word 'geology' put me off. Hera had wanted to follow the nature trail on the island, but, because of the students, Todd and the clownish Carbridge, I decided to push on to Rowardennan, which was our next stopping-place.

This part of our walk was rewarding but, along one shortish stretch, it was also hazardous, for it debouched on to a narrow, hilly, winding road with blind bends around which cars could give unwary walkers an unpleasant surprise. Some of the walk was up and down quite considerable slopes, but some of it was along the side of the loch. Hera sang and, if I knew the tune, I whistled it. We were very happy. The holiday was going to be a success, after all.

Inland, we passed through natural woods as well as through more of the Forestry Commission's plantations. Now and again we loitered at one or other of the small beaches which we came to beside the water. We also stopped to look at the views ahead and astern of us and, as we walked on, we could look across the loch to the motor-road which ran along on the other side past Tarbet and Ben Vorlich and on to Ardlui.

Sometimes we paddled in the shallows or sat and tossed stones into the water. One way and another we walked or idled away the time and ate some of the food we had bought in Drymen. Altogether it was a very easy-going, pleasant day. The weather was perfect but not unduly hot, the oak woods through which we passed were magnificent and so were the views when we came again into the open country or on to the shore of the loch.

All that day we found that the markers which charted The Way were well posted and easy to follow. The sign was a thistle inside a hexagon and there were also unmistakeable yellow arrows on signposts where The Way diverged from what appeared to be the obvious path.

We were so happy that, where this was possible, we walked hand-in-hand, more like children than like a sensible couple who had planned to test the temperature of a possible future together. I had begun to have my doubts at the outset of the walk, but they were all resolved on that halcyon day when we trekked from Balmaha to Rowardennan, where we were booked in at the youth hostel.

The magic in the air came from the weather and the scenery, of course, but, even so, I had learnt something of value to me. Hera and I could expect to have our ups and downs, a rough passage at times, frustrations and disagreements, but there would also be compensations, 'port after stormy seas', a benign providence somewhere in the offing, the isles of the blest for a safe anchorage at the end of the day. How one deceives oneself!

The youth hostel at Rowardennan was backed by trees and a hill, had a curious little turret and was beautifully situated on the shore of the loch. It had a hundred beds, served meals from Easter to September and there was also a members' kitchen, but it was very much more convenient for us to buy a meal there and conserve our emergency rations.

Ben Vrackie was away to our right as we faced the hostel, and the huge bulk of Ben Lomond loomed ahead. We were booked for two nights at Rowardennan and next morning nothing would satisfy Hera but to take the ferry across Loch Lomond to Inverbeg. It was running, so, together with a number of other hostellers — although none of them, so far as I could see, were acquaintances of ours — we boarded the boat.

Once ashore, we had lunch in Inverbeg and then walked along the road which follows the river through Glen Douglas. We crossed the railway and reached the Garelochhead–Arrocher road where, thanks, I think, to Hera's beauty, we thumbed a lift to Oban by way of Inverary on Loch Fyne and the Pass of Brander.

I had to hire a car and a driver to take us back to Inverbeg and we missed the boat on its return journey and had to spend the night at Inverbeg and cross back again in the morning.

'I wish we could stay here another night,' said Hera, when we stepped ashore at Rowardennan again. I felt the same urge and, in any case, I wanted to explain why we had not taken up our option of bedding down at the hostel the night before. We knew we were not the only hostellers who had crossed the loch on the previous day and some thoughtful soul had reported to the warden that we had missed the boat. I asked whether we could stay an extra night. The hostel was not full, so permission was readily granted and we spent most of the daylight hours on the little loch-side beach in front of the hostel, except for part of the afternoon when we took another trip on the water to the head of the loch and back.

It would have been possible to follow the example of some of the other hostellers and climb Ben Lomond, a scheduled half-day excursion by a well-established route, but we decided upon a lazy day instead, as there would be enough walking to do before we reached Fort William and Ben Nevis.

Part of our time on the beach was spent watching canoeists, for the place is the centre for the Scottish Youth Hostels' canoe club. We could have gone trout-fishing, had we wished, for permits were available. However, the long, lazy daylight hours suited our contented mood and I do not know when I have spent a pleasanter or more relaxing time. Hera had one complaint, but she voiced it with a smile.

'It's a lovely holiday,' she said, 'but everything is going much too well. It isn't testing our relationship at all.' Obviously she had forgotten any strained feelings after we had left the airport hotel.

'Give it time,' I said. 'We haven't got to Crianlarich yet, let alone to the edge of Rannoch Moor and the Devil's Staircase.'

'I shall be glad to be on the move again tomorrow,' she said.

'Even if that other lot are walking all the way from Milngavie,' (we had been told to pronounce it Milguy), 'they can't be all that far behind us now. We've spent a lot of time on The Way. I know we must have passed them early on, but they'll be catching up with us soon.'

I had forgotten Carbridge and his press-gang.

'Heavens, yes,' I said. 'It reminds me of *An Inland Voyage*, when I think of the possibility of running into that lot again.'

'Well, this isn't an inland voyage so far,' said Hera. 'We've been more or less beside Loch Lomond all the time and we even crossed it yesterday.'

'I meant Stevenson's book. He and his friend met some Belgian canoeists who more or less invited them to canoe with the local champion, who would make himself available if they would wait until the Sunday. They didn't. They sneaked off. He says, "And, indeed, it was not time for scruples; we seemed to feel the hot breath of the champion on our necks." Now that you have mentioned Carbridge, I seem to feel his hot breath on mine. We'll leave first thing in the morning.'

We were unlucky. The gang, some of them looking extremely jaded, turned up just as we left the beach that evening to go into the hostel for supper. The person who showed no sign of fatigue was the effervescent Carbridge. He came in with Todd and was shouting loudly and gleefully to him as they entered, 'And where did *you* get to last night, you sly moonlighter? Trust a don to find a donah, eh, you *hidalgo*, you! And, damme, look who's here, old boy, old boy!'

Well, it is not possible to leg it into a youth hostel and make a dash for your own room or to have your own separate table for meals. As soon as we appeared, we were seized upon by Carbridge and the others and found that it was impossible to escape. For what remained of the evening, including the supper-time, we were unwilling listeners to stories of the adventures, mishaps and triumphs of the party as they had made their way from Milngavie to Rowardennan. Only the hostel rules of lights out and silence broke up the gathering and cut short the flow.

Carbridge made one more attempt to persuade us to join the

rest of them on the walk. When it failed he said, 'Well, if you can't join us, beat us. I challenge you, old boy, old boy.'

'To what?'

'That we'll reach Fort William before you do.'

'I don't know that we're bothering about Fort William. We shall probably knock off at Kinlochleven,' I told him. 'The rest of The Way is over an old military road, I believe, and might not be very interesting.'

'Make it Kinlochleven, then, although, if you end up there, you'll be missing the best part of the trip.'

'I think not, from what I've heard and read.'

'It's a first-class YH at Fort William and we shall climb Ben Nevis from there. You'll be missing all that.'

'I wish you the joy of it.'

'Well, five quid that at least two of us, me and a lassie, as they say in these parts, get to Kinlochleven before you two do. Walking all the way, of course. No more of this bus and train lark of yours. Am I on?'

'No, of course you're not. If we fancy taking to the public transport, we shall do just that.'

'Cissy stuff, old boy, old boy.'

'I'm glad you didn't accept the bet openly,' said Hera, when we had seen the gang off next morning, 'but, all the same, we *will* get to Kinlochleven before they do. Him and a lassie indeed! I'm a better walker than any of these women he's got with him, I'm certain of that, and I'm going to prove it.'

'But we may feel the urge to take a bus or train here and there. The weather may change. We may get blisters on our feet or even sprain an ankle. All sorts of things could happen.'

'So they could to Carbridge and the others. Look here, Comrie, if I had been one of your men friends you wouldn't have turned down that bet.'

'Yes, I should. Under no circumstances am I prepared to go into any sort of a huddle with that irritating blighter. Anyway, although I told him we were only going as far as Kinlochleven, of course we're finishing at Fort William. All the same, I'm going to see that we hang about long enough to make sure that he's left Fort William before we get there. I'm not going to run into that gang again if I can possibly help it. Of all the boring evenings I've ever spent, last night was the worst.'

'Kinlochleven is not a place to hang about in. Isn't it all factories and works and things?'

'We can cross by the Ballachulish Bridge, then, and not go into Kinlochleven at all. We don't have to stick to The Way.'

She said no more, but I knew, by the obstinate set of her chin, that if she had her say, we were to walk The Way to Kinlochleven come hail, wind, physical injury, rain or snow.

I had seen the others loading up with food at Rowardennan, so it looked as though they were going to bivouac on the way. There was little chance that we should catch up with them, I thought, at any rate on the first stage of the journey. It was only just over seven miles to Inversnaid and they had set off at half past eight from the hostel, so I guessed that they would pass the burn and the waterfall and be well on their way to Inverarnan before they rested and had their lunch. We ourselves had decided upon a mid-morning snack and a drink at Inversnaid, where there was a very good hotel. We were also booked in for the night there — separately again, of course.

It was a place I had seen once before, but not when I had been walking The Way. My mother and father had taken me on a coach tour when I was very young and we had followed the Glasgow to Arrochar road to turn off for Glencoe. The lunch stop had been at the Inversnaid hotel, however, and to reach it we had to be ferried across the loch and then back again in the afternoon to rejoin the coach.

As I recall it, the boat was supplied by the hotel and to get into it we had to step up on to an empty petrol can. I could not remember the lunch or anything about the hotel except that I saw two young men drop a large, heavy crate of eggs just outside the entrance. They stood and roared with laughter at the extremely messy result. I think they must have been Irishmen come over for the summer season to provide extra help at the hotel, for I cannot believe that Scotsmen, even Highlanders, would have regarded such a wasteful catastrophe with such uninhibited joy. We laughed, too, of course. Such laughter is really rooted in shock.

I particularly wanted Hera to see the waterfall. It is immensely high and so early in the summer there would be a lot of water coming down. Wordsworth admired the torrent, but, when we came upon it after having heard it from a long way off, Hera quoted from Gerard Manley Hopkins:

> ' "This darksome burn, horseback brown,
>    His rollrock highroad roaring down
>    In coop and in coomb the fleece of his foam
>    Flutes and low to the lake falls home," '

she said, gazing at the tumbling torrent with the fascination I had hoped for.

We came upon it rather unexpectedly, as a matter of fact, in spite of the noise it made. We had had rather a rough scramble after walking through woods and then along the side of the loch, but, coming through more woodland on another stretch of The Way, we had seen birds and wild flowers which enchanted both of us and the sound of the waterfall was a diapason to all this happiness.

When we came in sight of the torrent and Hera had spoken Hopkins' lines, I put my arm round her and quoted in her ear:

> 'What hand but would a garland cull
>    For thee who art so beautiful?'

'Then why didn't you cull me one?' she asked. 'There was plenty of opportunity a little while ago.'

We knew that by now we must be well in the rear of Carbridge and his party, and by the time we had spent the night at the Inversnaid hotel they would be miles and miles ahead of us. They had camping gear with them and, as there was no sign of them at Inversnaid, I guessed that they would pitch tents somewhere near Inverarnan before going on to the youth hostel at Crianlarich. I thought it possible that the two clerks might opt for a night at a hotel, but not any of the others.

After lunch, Hera and I climbed a winding road up Glen Arklet past the little loch of the same name which is the property of the Glasgow waterworks and, to my mind, most uninteresting, but we did not finish the walk and reach Loch Katrine. Hera wanted to do this, but I pointed out that by the time we got there and back we should have added at least ten miles to the seven and a quarter we had already covered between Rowardennan and Inversnaid and that we still had to get to Crianlarich the next day.

She gave in, but rather resentfully.

'It's a great pity to miss the Trossachs when we're so close,' she said. I pointed out that, even if we reached Loch Katrine, we could not reach the Trossachs without circumambulating most of the loch. She was silent at this. However, she admitted at dinner that I had been right and we went to our separate rooms at peace with one another.

I had a job to get her away from the waterfall after breakfast on the following morning, but we were on the move at last in perfect weather and before the day was too hot.

Hardly had we set out for Inverarnan, however, than she embarked upon a discussion of our marriage from an angle which surprised and annoyed me.

'Comrie,' she said, 'I don't want to have to sign myself Hera Melrose.'

'Well, marry some other bloke, then,' I said lightheartedly, thinking that she was teasing me.

'Don't be silly! Look, your firm is called Alexander Comrie, isn't it?'

'Alexander for Sandy, the senior partner, Comrie for me. We thought it sounded better for a literary agency than Storey and Melrose. What about it? Lots of firms do the same sort of thing. It's quite legal, so long as you register the name.'

'But, Comrie, you have another name, haven't you?'

'Yes. You know I have. It's Alan.'

'I wouldn't mind being Mrs Alan Comrie.'

'Well, you can't be that, if you marry me. My name is Alan Comrie Melrose.' I began to wonder what she was getting at.

It did not sound like teasing, after all.

'Is Comrie a real Christian name?'

'Not being a Christian I can't say.' But she was not to be fobbed off by persiflage of that sort.

'You know what I mean,' she said shortly.

'Comrie was the surname of the uncle who left me such money as I have put into the firm.'

'Well, wouldn't he be pleased if he knew you had adopted Comrie as your own surname?'

'I shouldn't think he'd bother to sit up in his grave and cheer. Anyway, Melrose I am, and Melrose I stay.'

In that extraordinary way of hers, she realised that, although I tried not to show it, she had annoyed me. She abandoned the subject completely except to say, with a promise I could not mistake, that whoever would view fair Melrose aright must visit it by pale moonlight. I was not sure that she was quoting quite correctly, but I knew that she was offering me a bribe. Alan Comrie I was to agree to become. I said no more; neither did she. On our way from Inversnaid, we came upon a family of otters gorging themselves on the waste food thrown out from the hotel. They took not the slightest notice of us, so I am in great hopes that nobody hunts them in those parts.

We did not bother to visit Rob Roy's Cave. In any case it is not, as Hera pointed out, a 'real' cave, but a fissure in the rocks. Moreover, we had learned from the brochure that some idiot had marked it in large white letters and so destroyed any romance which could ever have been attached to it. I don't wonder that Stonehenge and other fascinating monuments to the past have had to be protected from the many-headed.

The next mile or two made very rough walking indeed. We scrambled and toiled towards Inverarnan, sometimes through woods, sometimes along the lochside. There was a bonus in the form of a wild goat, but we gave it as wide a berth as we could. Once, on the Isle of Wight, I had freed a domesticated goat which had got its tether wound round a gorse bush, and the horned, ungrateful devil had then done its best to rush at me and butt me into the sea.

Apart from the goat, the only interest lay in our struggles to keep our footing on the rough path while we listened to the traffic on the other side of the loch. At Doune, or rather just before we reached a desolate farmhouse on the way to that place, we took a break on a gravel shore and then, after we had crossed a brook, the going became easier and we stopped to take a look at some deserted farm buildings.

From Doune (one of three places of that name in Scotland) to Inverarnan the way was easy. We climbed, rested, and then went by way of a little pass to find a glorious view of the loch we were leaving behind us with Ben Lomond guarding it. Ahead of us were other great mountains — I think Ben Lui was one. Soon we dropped downhill, partly through woodland, until we came to a bridge. A ruined farm and a waterfall led us to another bridge, this one over the River Falloch. After that, we came out on to the main road and so to the hotel.

I went inside to confirm our booking, secure in the knowledge that, if we ever ran into Carbridge and the others again, it would not be at Inverarnan. Neither was it. That unwished-for joy awaited us at Crianlarich, although that bit of information was not given us until we got there.

Blessed is he that expecteth nothing, runs the writ to which Gilbert Keith Chesterton too optimistically added, 'for he shall be gloriously surprised'. In my experience, the glorious surprises have always been leaked beforehand, for it is not only bad news which travels fast. Our bad news did not travel at all, in one sense. It simply caught up with us, but that came later, for at Inverarnan, except for the prospect yet again of separate beds, all was well and I felt remarkably fit and very happy as I went to the hotel desk, leaving Hera outside.

# 3

# *A Change in the Weather*

It was as I came out again that I saw the gypsy. She was an old woman with a keen face and wispy grey hair coming from under a man's felt hat.

'Mind how you go, my pretty,' she said to Hera. We stopped, although I hardly know why. She had sprigs of flowering rowan in her basket and some fronds of young bracken. Colour was provided by a collection of paper flowers, red, blue, yellow and mauve.

'Mind how I go? Why?' asked Hera, although I touched her arm to indicate that we should move on. I wanted to have a look round before we dined.

'The Way is long,' said the gypsy.

> ' "The wind was cold,
>    The minstrel was infirm and old," '

I quoted, and gave another slight touch to Hera's arm.

'You keep to The Way,' said the gypsy, ignoring me. 'It may be long, but there is danger if you stray. Buy a flower and a bit of green fern, lady. Green is a lucky colour for you. Buy a bit of rowan for the white soul of you. Come autumn, there will be berries red as pigeons' blood, but the flower of the rowan, that's white as milk, as pure as your heart, my lady.'

'All right,' said Hera. She picked a spray of rowan out of the gypsy's basket and gave the old woman a fifty pence coin. 'Now tell me why I'm to mind how I go. Go where?'

'Come you apart from your gentleman.'

I was not very keen on this, but Hera motioned me to stay where I was. The gypsy took her aside far enough for me to be out of earshot. The conference was not a very long one. Hera came back to me with a couple of paper flowers as well as the spray of rowan for which she had paid such a ridiculously exorbitant price, but she refused to disclose any details of the conversation.

'It's all a lot of nonsense, I expect,' she said. 'Let's go and look at the old canal.'

I saw that it would be useless for a time to ask any questions, but I guessed that she would come out with something later on. I spent a comfortable night, although I had no luck, as I say, with the sleeping arrangements because I had booked us in separately again at Hera's insistence. I hoped she now regretted this as much as I did, but, short of telling them at the desk that we had got married since I had made the booking, there was nothing to be done about it.

We breakfasted at eight next day and went back to join The Way, but midway through the stop we made for our elevenses Hera came up with one of those bright ideas which might seem all right at the time, but end in disaster later.

'You've got maps, haven't you?' she said.

'Sure. Why?' I asked, scenting danger.

'When we get to Crianlarich we'll study the map,' said the temptress. 'There might be a short cut we could take. So long as we don't use public transport, nothing was said about having to keep strictly to The Way, was it?'

'No, but I didn't accept any bets and one doesn't take short cuts in this sort of country unless one is a fool or has been born and brought up here.'

'Oh, we won't take a short cut unless it's marked on the map,' she said.

'Well, it won't be. The Way would follow it if it were.'

'We'll see,' she said. Again, I did not argue. There were nearly seven miles to cover before we reached Crianlarich and I thought she would have forgotten about short cuts by the time we got there.

From Inverarnan to Crianlarich we were in Glen Falloch and had left Loch Lomond behind. We finished on the old military road constructed, I suppose, by Wade, who opened up parts of the Highlands in this way to assist in what was known as their pacification. This meant he had to move his troops about to get to the trouble spots during and after the Jacobite risings.

It was when we had left the river we had been following and were getting near our destination that we caught up with the first of Carbridge's off-loadings. These were Perth and the students. One could not call them stragglers, since they had fallen behind only in order to get on with the job they had come to do. They were all busy with notebooks, maps, chisels and their little geological hammers and told us that they were having a great time and had booked beds at the youth hostel in Crianlarich, where they hoped to see us again.

We gave them our good wishes and asked how far ahead the rest of the party would be. It turned out that they had all booked in at the hostel, but Carbridge might have decided to push on towards Tyndrum without stopping in Crianlarich.

'He must be mad,' said Hera. 'The hostel at Crianlarich is the last one on The Way until he gets to Fort William.'

'He talked of camping and how much time they would save that way because they would be striking camp at the crack of dawn each day. I'm thinking we delayed the rest of them an unco' time on Inchcailloch and he is impatient to be pushing on. Ye'll mind ye of the lassies Green and Parks?' said Perth.

'Would those be Rhoda and Tansy?' I asked.

'The same. They canna thole yon man Carbridge, I'll be thinking, and they are to leave the rest of us and take to the train, but whether they will then go on to Fort William I dinna ken.'

'When did they leave the party?'

'They are bookit in at Crianlarich the night, sensible lassies, so we'll meet up wi' them there.'

'We'll meet them there, too, and you and the students, of course.'

'Aye. We can do wi' a bed the night, for we shall be into the hills the morn, and that may be hard going for the lassies, wi' the digging and scraping and all.'

'Does that mean you will spend more than tomorrow prospecting around these parts?'

'We're biding three nights. The students are awfu' keen and we're a wee thing weary o' yon man Carbridge and his haverings.'

'We soon got bored with him, too. I don't know much about geology, so what are the students actually looking for in these parts?'

'We didna let on to the rest of them, but you and Miss Camden are sensible bodies, so I'll tell ye. Ye'll mind ye of a theory that, awa' back in time, the geography of the world was vastly different from the way it is today? Well, what these laddies and lassies are after is to match the American dinosaurs wi' bones found over on this side. There is muckle talk o' the Cretaceous period and its giant sauropods — '

'Titanosaurus from Argentina,' I said. 'Go back to the Jurassic and we get Brachiosaurus, who was also four-footed, but during the Cretaceous time we also get Tyrannosaurus. He seems to have walked upright on massive hind legs and his forelegs were tiny and can't have been of much use for any practical purpose. The Americans found a good specimen of this intimidating chap in Montana, I believe, and the Russians found another one in Mongolia.'

'I thought ye kenned nothing about geology.'

'Oh, everybody is interested in dinosaurs.' We wished the working party luck again, said we would see them at the hostel supper and that we were leaving after next morning's breakfast.

'We must get provisions in Crianlarich if we are going to take a short cut across country,' said Hera, when we came in sight of the hostel.

'There are not going to be any short cuts. It's crazy to think of such a thing,' I said in my firmest tones.

'We shall see,' she said again, putting out her tongue at me.

The hostel was in a turning off the Tarbet–Crianlarich road and, further on, the turning led to the road between Tyndrum and Killin. A disused railway line was just beyond it.

The hostel itself was described by Hera as quaint. It was in two parts. One part was raised above the ground on piers. The entrance was up some steps to a building just behind the other. There were sixty-four beds, a members' kitchen and a hostel store, but meals were not provided, so that conditioned our shopping. We went back with the food for the next day, but bought our supper from the hostel shop.

On enquiry of the warden at the hostel we learned that although Carbridge and his party had not cancelled their booking, they had not yet arrived. Perth and the students, as they had told us, were booked in for three nights. The office girls were booked in, too, but did not turn up, so we assumed that they had decided to take the train straightaway and we did not expect to see them again unless they were at the hostel in Fort William when we arrived there.

It looked as though Carbridge's party had been reduced to four, himself and Todd and the brother and sister Jane and James Minch, but Perth that evening gave it as his opinion that the couple would leave The Way after Tyndrum, as Jane was footsore and James had quarrelled with Todd.

'The quarrel was about Jane, I suppose,' said Hera. 'I don't trust men where girls are concerned.' But it was at me she looked. I laughed, and she went on: 'Never mind that. We've got to pass Carbridge as soon as possible. If he's got the two Minches in tow and poor Jane Minch with sore feet, we may be able to pass him between Tyndrum and Bridge of Orchy. After all the walking they've done, even Todd and Carbridge may be inclined to slow down a bit from now on.'

'We shall never pass them if they're camping and we are staying the night at a hotel,' I said. 'They'll be away at first light and I'm certainly not going to get up at dawn and miss my breakfast. Who cares about Carbridge when a Scottish breakfast is in the offing?'

'You are a pig where food is concerned!'

I grinned and told her to bear the fact in mind when we were married. All the same, I resented the unnecessary slur and said I would go for a walk. I strolled out with the intention of taking a look at the route we should be taking next day. I walked alongside the loch, but had not gone far when I met the Minch brother and sister. Jane was limping. I stopped.

'I thought you were pushing on,' I said. James indicated his sister.

'We thought the same,' he said, 'but Jane can't go any further without something being done about her feet. Like lunatics, we've brought no first-aid stuff except a crêpe bandage and some of those bits you stick on to cuts. We're going back to the hostel to see whether we can pick up something more useful.'

'I've got stuff,' I said, 'and she's done enough walking.' With this, I picked up the slightly-built girl and carried her like a baby. When we got to the hostel, I produced my kit and ministered to her small, tender feet. I knew all this would irritate Hera and it did, but I found I did not care. Looking after Jane was like caring for a child. I found it a pleasant experience. Her brother then took her up to bed.

Perth and the students arrived a bit later and the youngsters soon turned in, but Perth still stayed up. Looking out of the window he said, 'Losh! Look who's here!' It was Carbridge and Todd. They had noticed that the weather was changing and, as they had not cancelled their booking at the hostel, they had decided to go back on their tracks and seek beds instead of camping out.

Hera congratulated them upon their common sense, at which Carbridge said, 'Your commendation, fair one, is as the voice of the turtle dove,' and he began to sing, as he showed signs of putting his arm around Hera:

> 'If the heart of a man is depressed with cares,
>     the mist is dispelled when a woman appears.'

I did not allow him to finish. I leapt from my chair and choked the song into guttural incoherence by clutching his throat.

'That's enough of that, old boy, old boy!' I said savagely. 'Don't push your luck!' I flung him aside and he caught his heel and sat down hard on the floor. Perth took my arm.

'Get ye to bed, man,' he said. I looked at Hera, but she was looking at Todd.

Todd said to her, 'This is no place for you. Now this has happened, you might be better off staying at the hotel for the night. Let me take you over to it and book you in. I was even thinking of taking a room there myself.'

'Belt up!' I said, furious with myself to find that I was shaking. 'If she needs to stay in the hotel — '

'All right, all right. Message received and understood,' he said. 'Don't get your underpants in a twist. It was only a suggestion.'

'Then keep the next one to yourself,' I shouted. Hera turned her back on me.

Carbridge picked himself up. 'Well, really!' he said, dusting the seat of his trousers. 'No need for that, old boy, old boy.' He made for the men's dormitory, for which the students had already left the common-room. I suppose he had decided he wanted no part in a further rough-house.

Perth took me by the sleeve again and said, 'We're all a wee thing weary, I'm thinking. The laddie meant no harm. Ye'll see it in perspective come the morn's morn.' Before going to bed, however, I insisted on having it out with Todd.

The party of four were off at eight the next day. Hera and I breakfasted together, but it was a silent meal. The weather had held up, after all, and I wished with all my heart that Carbridge and the others could have known that it would, and had held on their way instead of returning to the hostel. The warden was not very friendly when I collected our membership cards, so I guessed that some account of the happenings had leaked out, although nobody but the people concerned had been present at the time of my outburst.

Perth and the students had also gone out early and Hera and I were off by nine. The walk was by way of Strath Fillan through forest and across a river. Then we were out on the moors with the mountains hemming us in. As the road to Tyndrum began to rise, we could look back at Ben More and Stobinian, and as we looked ahead we had a view of Ben Challum before the track sloped downwards to a stream.

The Way climbed again after that and, as we had made good

time since leaving Crianlarich, I warned Hera that we had better look out for Carbridge and his party, but when we got to the bridge on the River Fillan and had had a look at the ruins of St Fillan's Chapel a bit further on, there was still no sign of them.

In a village called Clifton — after a property magnate who had the right to mine the lead which was discovered near the place at some time in the eighteenth century — we found a shop which stocked food, so we replenished our own stores before going on. As we reached Tyndrum, I looked up at the sky and decided that Carbridge had not been so far wrong the night before. 'I'll ask at the hotel whether they can have us here for a night.'

'Oh, no, you won't. We're going to catch Carbridge and pass him without his knowing it. He can't possibly be far in front of us now if he's got poor Jane Minch hanging on to him. All we need is that short cut I mentioned.'

'I had no idea you were so obstinate,' I said.

'I am not obstinate. I have made up my mind that we are going to get to Fort William before he does, that's all. After that exhibition you made of yourself last night, the least you can do is to help me over racing him to the finish.'

'I told him we were packing up at Kinlochleven,' I said weakly. 'I don't know why he gets my goat to the extent he does. If he weren't such a worm, perhaps his stupid talk and the liberties he tries to take with you wouldn't rile me so much.'

'It was you who took the liberties. You made me look an utter fool. Thank goodness that spotty little Minch girl wasn't present. She might have thought you the big, bold hero.'

'Freckles are not spots.'

'Yes, they are. The other name for them is sunspots.'

I tried to laugh, but she had not finished, so I tried to divert her from her criticism of my conduct of the night before by quoting Shakespeare. 'All right, they are sunspots,' I said.

> ' "The cowslips tall her pensioners be;
>    In their gold coats spots you see;
>    These be rubies, fairy favours — " '

'Oh, be quiet!' she said impatiently. 'What on earth induced you to behave like a jealous goat last night?'

'You know as well as I do. I'm not prepared to stand by and watch one oaf trying to put an arm round you and listen to another oaf offering to take you to a hotel for the night.'

'As for the first oaf, I could have managed him quite easily. I certainly didn't need *your* protection. As for Todd — well, I noticed you didn't try to choke the life out of *him*.'

'He's bigger than I am,' I said.

At that her mood changed. She laughed. 'I know what's really the matter with you,' she said. 'It's this enforced abstinence. However, we agreed on a celibate holiday and we're sticking to it. I don't suppose holding Jane Minch in your arms was much of a comfort, was it?'

'You would be surprised,' I said.

It was about half a dozen miles, or perhaps seven, from Tyndrum to Bridge of Orchy and we were following an old military road. It seemed easy going after some of the country we had passed through and we made good progress. We were not intending to break our journey at Bridge of Orchy anyway, but I still did not much like the look of the weather, although the view from the top of the hill had been fairly clear.

'What are all those posts?' asked Hera, after the road had descended from the hill.

'Snow posts. Very handy guides in winter or if a Highland mist comes down.' As though, by mentioning it, I had conjured it up, we had not reached the tiny settlement before a heavy mist blotted out everything except a short stretch of the road in front of us.

'There's a hotel at Bridge of Orchy,' I said. 'We'd better book in as soon as we get to it. If this mist means anything, we shall probably get rain, and I'm not walking in wet clothes if I can help it.'

'Sugar baby!'

'It's you I'm thinking about.'

'Yes,' she said, to my surprise, 'I really believe it was.'

As we approached Bridge of Orchy, the mist lifted and there were views which were not to be missed. We crossed a bridge and the railway came under the slopes of Beinn Doran on to an old road and then alongside a river. It was still easy walking and we loitered and I smoked while Hera gazed at the glen through which the river ran and the mountains which we were approaching.

We had spent so much time on this part of The Way that we decided to lunch at the Bridge of Orchy hotel before going on to Inveroran. The mist kept off, we had a fairly late and leisurely lunch and it was well past mid-afternoon by the time we took to The Way again and were headed for our overnight stop.

I took another look at the sky when we had left the hotel and did not much like what I saw, for the mountains were already beginning to be shrouded and I fancied that there was rain in the air. I began to wish that we had ended the day's journey at Bridge of Orchy and felt that I ought to have insisted on this, but foolishly I had agreed to let Hera try her short cut. Anyway, it seemed more sensible to do the extra bit of walking on the one day and so reduce the next day's stage to nine and a half miles instead of a dozen. Although Hera boasted of her fitness, I thought that mile after mile, day after day, was quite sufficient test of her capabilities.

For a long time that day our track had been running more or less beside the railway, but after Bridge of Orchy we knew we would lose both the railway and the main road. We expected to pick up the road at Kingshouse, for which we should be headed when we left Inveroran, but we would not see the railway again until we reached Fort William.

After about half an hour the mountains became nothing but looming, shadowy masses, amorphous giants, spectral, although not, so far, menacing. All the same, I began to appreciate the stories current in the Highlands of spooky manifestations and was only too willing to believe in witches, terrifying water-horses and all the rest of the legends and old wives' tales.

I knew, too, that we must soon be on the fringes of Rannoch Moor, that wilderness of peat-bogs, water, heather and evil repute, but it was when I became aware that we must have

covered a good deal more than the two and a half miles between
Bridge of Orchy and Inveroran that it was borne in upon me
that, with the mist thickening every minute, we must, at some
time after leaving the village, have deviated from the signposted
Way.

It was Hera who gave voice to my misgivings by observing
that it seemed a long time since my torch, which I had needed
to switch on, had picked out any markers.

'I suppose we're on the right track?' she said.

'I've been wondering that,' I answered. 'Perhaps we'd better
go back to the village. It's easy to get lost in a mist like this, and
I'm beginning to think we've gone wrong somewhere.'

'Oh, no, don't let's go back. We're on a route of some sort. It
must lead somewhere. Besides, we might not strike the road
back. If we're lost now, we could get lost again and might be
worse off than we are at present. I'm sorry I ever mentioned a
short cut. I don't somehow think this is one.'

# 4

## *Shelter — at a Price*

There seemed no doubt that we were out on Rannoch Moor and my heart began to fail me. Who could tell what treacherous morass or small but dangerous lochan awaited us? It was all right, I supposed, so long as we could keep to what must, in old time, have been a drover's road, or perhaps a stretch of a military road long since abandoned or, possibly, never completed, but what was to happen to us if, at some time, it petered out or if our legs refused to allow us to walk any further? It was not as though we were seasoned hikers accustomed to bad weather and other hazards. We had nothing with which to make camp or any other kind of bivouac. Hera guessed what I was thinking and spoke cheerfully and with optimism.

'We've got food, thank goodness,' she said, 'and this track may be rough, but it seems firm enough. I expect it leads to a bothy or a disused shepherd's hut. There will be some sort of shelter where we can lie up until the mist clears.'

'I'm very sorry I've landed you in this,' I said. 'I ought to have realised ages ago that we'd come off The Way.'

'Why do you blame yourself? It's my fault. If I'd listened to you, we should have been safe and snug at Bridge of Orchy. You're right. I *am* obstinate and wrong-headed. You should be firmer with me.'

'Some hopes! You're a law unto yourself.'

'Oh, well, I suppose this is our testing-time and we shall have to survive it. It may prove to be a blessing in disguise. Who knows?'

As though her optimism had wrought some sort of magic, shelter came halfway to meet us, as it were, for we almost walked into a wall. Just in time, the torch I was using picked out the obstacle. I put out my hand. It met rough stone and my torch, which had warned me, showed us great slabs of what looked like granite.

'If there's a wall, there must be a door,' I said. We groped our way to the right and, at thirty stumbling paces, found an opening. 'Stand still while I explore. When you hear me call out, switch on your torch so that I can find you again.' (We had agreed not to use her torch unless this was absolutely necessary, because we did not know when we would be able to buy any more batteries.)

'Don't be long, then,' she said. 'What do you think this place is?'

'Goodness knows.' I left her and felt my way along the wall until my hand suddenly encountered nothingness. I stopped short and shone my torch into what seemed a man-made aperture. I groped my way in, picked out another wall, felt my way along it and moved the torch up and down. Suddenly I found that I was looking at an unglazed window. It was not very large and it was rounded at the top. I groped my way back to Hera, but caught my foot on a chuck of stone, fell and hit my head. I picked myself up and got to her, but felt rather dizzy.

'I think it's a house of sorts,' I said, 'but I doubt whether it's occupied. I've found an entrance and a window, but there's no glass in it and I couldn't see any lights. There must be a door further on. Mind how you go. It's a bit rough underfoot.' I felt my head, but it was not bleeding.

With her at my heels, I moved forward again. Then I stopped, after warning her that I was going to do so, and shone my torch in at the glassless window. It was as misty inside the building as outside it. I felt certain that the place, whatever it was, was empty, but I called out to ask whether anybody was at home.

There was no response, although I called out more than once, so I told Hera again to stay where she was while I tried to find a proper door to the building.

'If I can't,' I said, 'we shall have to scramble in through this window. Think you can manage?'

'If you can, I can. Why don't we do it? Even if you do find a door, it will probably be locked and I don't much want to be left alone here while you go exploring. Besides, you might fall down a well or some other awful thing, and then what should we do? Please let us stay together.'

There seemed common sense in this. I told her to pocket her torch and I handed her mine with instructions to light me while I scrambled in. Then I took the torch from her and, with my help, she managed the climb more easily than I had done.

We both used our torches when she had joined me inside, and found that we were in a dark bare room with a fireplace opposite the window. The roof was low and, so far as I could tell, it appeared to be sound.

'Thank God for that,' I said. 'We can roost here until the mist lifts.'

'What's the time?'

'Half five. We must have come a mighty long way since we left Bridge of Orchy.'

'If I didn't already know that, my legs would tell me,' she said. 'I couldn't walk another step until I've had a rest. We shan't see Inveroran tonight or any dinner. I'm going to get out of these wet things and put on my spares. You'd better do the same. The mist seeps into every kind of clothing.'

'If only we could make a fire,' I said, 'we could have a shot at drying our trousers and socks.' But, although there were ashes in the grate, there was no fuel. We ate some of our emergency rations and I set light to the paper bags in which the food had been packed, but they only flared up and, for an instant, showed not only more of the primitive bareness of the room, but an opening in one of the inside walls.

'We'll explore this place before we leave,' said Hera. 'I believe it's a ruined castle. All the same, I don't much want to spend the night here. If only the mist would lift!'

There seemed nothing to do except settle down and wait, so this we did for what seemed a very long time. Then Hera, who (both of us having changed into dry clothes), had been stretched out on the floor with her head pillowed in my lap, sat up and

said, 'Oh, look, Comrie! The mist's lifting. I can see the outline
of the window. Let's go.'

'I'm as thirsty as Tantalus,' I said. 'Do you mind if I look
around for a well or a tap or something?'

'I'll come with you.'

'No need. I'll take your mug and bring you a drink of water if
I can find any which seems drinkable.'

'No. I'll come. I don't much like this place.'

I went to the aperture and looked out. The mist had given
place to steady, relentless rain, but there was daylight again and
I found myself looking out on to a small, paved yard with a
high, retaining wall. I could see the archway by which we had
groped our way into the yard and when I put my head out of
the window I could see another archway at the further side of
the enclosure. Hera joined me and I made way so that she could
look out.

'Yes, we *must* be in the ruins of a castle,' she said. 'That
means we are miles off our track. There is no mention of castle
ruins in the brochure, is there?'

'Not so far as I know. It's probably the remains of one of
General Wade's little forts.'

'How far do you think we walked after we left Bridge of
Orchy?' she asked.

'Difficult to say, but, what with the mist and the rough road,
probably not as far as it seemed.'

We turned away from the window and went through the
doorway into a room which was better lighted than the one we
had left, for it had only three walls. In the angle of two of these
there was a stair. I had my torch with me, so I shone it, but it
lighted only a few of the stone steps before the turn of the spiral
hid the next part of the flight.

'That looks exciting,' said Hera.

'You don't go up there,' I said. 'It could be unsafe. Let's try
through here.' There was a massive nail-studded door in the
staircase wall. I pushed it open. Hera peered in.

'But it's pitch-dark,' she said.

'It must be the passage which led to the kitchen. This must

be the entrance hall that we're in and there will be a pump in the kitchen, I expect,' I told her cheerfully.

We never carried drinks in our rucksacks because of the extra weight, so all we had had to quench our thirst was a half-pound bag of cherries with which we had finished our recent meal. I advanced into the opening and shone my torch so that the beam was straight ahead of me.

'No wonder it's dark in here,' I said. 'It's blocked at the other end.' It was as I said the words that I fell over the dead man who was sprawled across the passage.

'Change back into your other clothes as quickly as you can,' I said, when I had hustled Hera back to the room into which we had climbed. 'We don't want to get these togs soaked as well, and it's pouring with rain outside.'

'Why the hurry? What's the matter? Couldn't you get the blocked end of the passage open?' she asked, understandably surprised by the force I had used to get her back into the other room.

'I didn't try. We've got to get away from here as quickly as ever we can. Don't ask questions. Just get changed.'

'You've got to tell me why. Did you see a ghost in the passage? – or what?'

'Not a ghost, although there might be one in the future. There's a dead man in there. I kicked him. Now for heaven's sake shut up and get changed. There's no point in getting *two* sets of clothes soaked through.'

Shivering with distaste, we climbed into our damp trousers and gave our anoraks, which were waterproof, a final shake before we put them on. 'Now let's have a good look round and make sure we haven't left any traces to show that we were here,' I said.

'But why? The police will have to be told about – about *him*.'

'Not on your life! We only found the body by the merest accident. It is no business of ours if people get themselves killed in ruined forts and I'm damned if I'm going to get myself mixed up with Scottish law and procurator fiscals and all the rest of it.

What we've got to do is to step it out as soon as we leave here and trust to luck that we can find either Bridge of Orchy or Inveroran before dark. The mist is excuse enough if we get there late. We've got to alibi ourselves, don't you see?'

'But why? And why did you drag me away from the passage like that? I wouldn't have minded seeing a corpse.'

'We'll go through that opening in the hall where the wall's gone. It will be easier than scrambling through that window again,' I said. 'I'll tell you more later. Come on! Come on!' So we passed through another, smaller yard which was strewn with fallen masonry, crossed into the first yard and so out of the precincts by the postern door. The road was plain enough to follow. We headed on to it and I set a cracking pace as we left the ruins behind us.

'Oh, do slow down a bit,' said Hera, after about the first half-mile. 'We're walking as though the Devil himself is behind us.'

'Who knows that he isn't?' I said, slackening the pace; and then I gave her the bad news. 'The dead man was Carbridge,' I said, 'and he wasn't merely dead; he'd been murdered. That's why I hauled you away before you saw him.' She said nothing in response to this, but, from then on, she set the pace herself and there was no more talk about going to the police. All she said was: 'I didn't want it to happen that way.'

'What didn't you?' I asked foolishly.

'I did want to get to Fort William before he did, but now he can't get there at all. But, look here' — she slowed down and almost stopped walking — 'are you sure it was Carbridge? It couldn't have been, you know. I mean, how did he get there and where are the other three?'

'Lost in the mist, the same as we were. He must have lost contact with them somewhere or other on the moor. Perhaps they were too slow for him if Jane Minch's feet are hurting her.'

'Todd wouldn't have been slow. They would have gone on together, wouldn't they? Where is Todd?'

'Fleeing from justice, perhaps. I tell you Carbridge was murdered. I saw that he was. It looks to me as though Todd — '

'No! You are not to say that! It's wicked. You have no proof!'

'Sorry! No, of course I haven't. Now let's hurry on. I can't forget I had a row with Carbridge last night and there were witnesses. I can't afford to report his body to the police. How can I?'

'I hadn't thought of that,' she said, 'but it was only a passing tiff. It would never occur to anybody who was there that any thought of murder was in your mind.'

'It would never occur to anybody?' I repeated, but in the form of a query, not a statement. 'Well, if you're interested, I might as well tell you that it occurred to *me*. If I had been alone with him last night — '

'If you had been alone with him, the situation would never have arisen. Look here, I was right the first time about reporting what you saw. Don't you see that the body is bound to be found soon. I suppose they'll either take it to Fort William or to Stirling, but I really haven't a clue about these things and I simply don't want to know, but can't you see, Comrie, we *must* tell the police we found him. There'll be the most awful trouble if we don't, when it all comes out that we were in that ruin.'

'How *can* it come out? Even if it was discovered that we were there, there is nothing to prove that we saw the body. I didn't even touch him.'

'You fell over him. You accidentally kicked him. Bodies can bruise, even if they're dead.'

'Which proves what? Look, now, Hera, if you go to the police, you'll land us in a whole lot of trouble and we may be held up for days, even if we're not actually placed under suspicion. The first thing the police are going to ask is whether we knew the man.'

'We could say no to that.'

'And have them round up Todd and the rest of the gang and prove us to be liars? That would help a lot!'

'Oh, dear! I don't know *what* to do.'

'That doesn't sound like you. Anyway, when in doubt, do nothing and let Time pass. What did somebody call it? — masterly inactivity. That's our ticket and we can't afford to swop it for any other. Can't you see that?'

It must have been at about this point that the rain eased off and we could see further ahead of us than we had been able to do since leaving the ruins. I had an idea that we were approaching the spot where we had deviated from The Way. I heard voices and laughter. Hastily I dragged Hera into a dip in the moor and pulled her down among the soaking plants in the hollow.

'Keep quiet,' I whispered. 'If anybody spots us here, they'll only think of Lady Chatterley in the rain, but we mustn't be seen walking away from the ruins.'

The voices died in the distance. Cautiously I reconnoitred. There was nobody to be seen, so I pulled Hera to her feet and hand in hand, muddy now as well as wet, we ran forward. Almost the first thing we set eyes on was one of the signs used to mark The Way.

'So this is where we went wrong,' she said. 'Just our luck! How do you *know* Carbridge was murdered?'

'Saw a dirty great knife sticking out of him. It was something I didn't want *you* to see.'

'And you're certain he was dead, although you didn't handle him?'

'Quite certain. He was cold and stiff.'

'Then you *must* have touched him, or you wouldn't have known that.'

'All right, I did touch him, but nobody will ever know, unless you tell them.'

'Oh, that's not fair!' she said passionately. 'Look here, I want to go home. I want to get on a train and go back to Glasgow, and then I want to get on another train and get to Euston, and then I want to take a taxi to my flat and never go on holiday again.'

'Cool it,' I said. 'Forget all about today. We've done nothing wrong and there certainly was nothing anybody could do for poor Carbridge. Let it ride. The most stupid thing we could do now is to go straight home. People would begin wondering why. When people begin wondering why, trouble starts.'

'What people?'

'People at home, for one thing. They would know we must have had some reason for cutting our holiday short and, naturally, they'd begin to speculate and then, once the body is discovered – '

'That might not be for ages, unless we – '

'Oh, my dear girl, use your loaf! The poor chap will be missed and a search will be made. Those ruins are not all that far off The Way and there are plenty of his gang to testify that he was walking The Way when he went missing. In fact, he will have been reported missing already, I wouldn't wonder. The sooner we get to Inveroran and pick up our planned schedule, the better. As it stands at present, nobody can prove that we ever deviated, let alone that we holed up in the ruins. The mist and the time we spent at Bridge of Orchy will account for that gap in the time scheme. Thank goodness we took so much time over lunch. It may turn out to be our alibi.'

'It still think we ought to go to the police.'

'In heaven's name, *no!* Do you want to land us both in the cart?'

'If he was murdered, the murderer ought to be found.'

'He *will* be found. No doubt about that.'

'Even a few hours may make all the difference.'

'Oh, Hera, it's no business of ours. Hang it all, we didn't even *like* the chap!'

'That's all the more reason for doing our best to see that justice is done.'

'Punishing his murderer won't bring Carbridge back.'

'Finding out who killed him may help a lot of people. Don't you see, Comrie, that one of his gang must have killed him? I wouldn't let you put it on to Todd, but *one* of that four – '

'Not necessarily at all. There are plenty of thugs and muggers about. He may have had a toss-up with the rest of them and gone off on his own and run into trouble.'

'Can you imagine that, though? He was the most gregarious pest I've ever met. He would never have gone off on his own.'

'Well, that could boil it down to just three people. So far as we know, he was left with Todd and the two Minches. Tansy and Rhoda had cried off and the students and Perth were way, way behind. Any of the other three could have had a reason for killing him. We don't know what the relationships were like among them.'

We tramped on, and were soon clocked in at the Inveroran hotel. No questions were asked about our wet and muddy appearance. They are used to wet and muddy people in the Highlands, I suppose. They promised that our clothes would be sponged and would be dry by the morning, so we went to our rooms, had a bath, changed (Hera into the slinky frock again), and went downstairs to have a drink before dinner. I began to relax, however temporarily.

Most of the other guests appeared to be climbers, and there was much talk of mountains I had never heard of, or else I did not recognise the pronunciation of their Gaelic names. We listened and admired and I hoped that our recent experiences were being overlaid in Hera's mind by pleasanter thoughts.

As the evening wore on, however, I myself again became very far from happy. I did not know much about rigor mortis, but I knew enough to realise that, if Carbridge were as stiff as I reckoned he was, he could have been dead for hours. This was very puzzling. I attempted to remember all that I had read about rigor mortis. My partner Alexander Storey and I run a literary agency which had been set up by Sandy's father and one or two of our clients write crime fiction, so, to that extent, I have had to undertake a certain amount of reading-up on forensic medicine in order to check the information given in the story before we send the book to a publisher.

To become as stiff as the corpse over which I had stumbled in that blacked-out passage, the man would have been dead for about twelve hours or even longer, for, so far as my recollection of my reading took me, the rigor, once completely established, could last another twelve hours until it began to pass off in the third twelve-hour period.

'It doesn't make sense,' I told myself. Carbridge had left the hotel at about eight that morning and I had found the body not more than ten hours later. Well, allowing for the individual vagaries of its onset, I supposed that it would have been just about possible for the corpse to have stiffened in that space of time, but the legs, with their powerful muscles, were always the last parts of the body to be affected, and it was his foot and leg that I had stumbled against and then touched. They had been as rigid as marble.

I had another try at working out the times. With Jane Minch in tow and her sore feet, Carbridge could not have travelled all that much faster than we did. We had stopped for lunch, but, presumably, so had the others. It did not seem possible that Carbridge could have been dead for more than a few hours. Further speculation seemed useless. I tried to tell myself that it was not Carbridge I had found, but it was of no use. True, I had had only a glimpse of a grossly distorted face, but the jeans and the anorak the man was wearing were identical to the clothes Carbridge had been wearing when last I had seen him alive.

# 5

# *The End of a Holiday*

It was between nine and ten miles to Kingshouse from Inveroran and, as the challenge from Carbridge could now be ignored by Hera, she agreed to make an easy business of next day's journey.

We left the hotel at half-past nine, and by the time we reached the beginning of the climb up the Black Mount when we left the head of Luch Tulla I realised that Hera was very tired. There seemed nothing to do but to press on or return to the Inveroran hotel, have lunch there and then try to get a lift in a car or lorry to carry us to Ballachulish, Kinlochleven or even all the way to Fort William itself.

When I suggested this, however, she vetoed it in such a forceful manner that I realised it was useless to argue, so we began the ascent. The surface of The Way on this stretch was good, but the track became extremely exposed and windy. However, the weather remained fine and the mountain views were wonderful and so was the expanse of Rannoch Moor we saw before we descended.

We rested for a while on Ba Bridge and watched the tumbling water as it swirled over its rocks brought down from the mountain crags, but there was more climbing to do and, although I stopped and pointed out a rough track which would have taken us to the road and the chance of a lift, Hera refused to consider the project and lowered her obstinate head to the wind as we looked over to where Schiehallion reared his noble pyramid out of the moor.

I have always thought about this extraordinary mountain ever since I first met its magical name in J. A. Ferguson's one-act play *Campbell of Kilmhor* and shall never forget the closing speech by the old woman Mary Stewart after the heroic and defiant death of her son Dugald. He told the despicable Campbell, 'Till ye talk Rannoch Loch to the top of Schiehallion, ye'll no talk me into a yea or nay.' Apart from that, it was during rehearsals of this play that I had fallen in love with Hera. She had been cast as the girl Morag Cameron, while I played the tiny part of the toadying and sycophantic James Mackenzie. Amateur material were the whole lot of us, but the play itself carried us through, although I wouldn't go bail for our Campbell's Scottish accent! However, I digress, as the lecturer said when he was extolling the beauties of the Clifton Blue butterfly and stepped backwards off the cliffs at Beachy Head.

Slowly, and with many pauses for rest, although it was too wet everywhere to sit down, we made progress towards Kingshouse. Of one thing I was determined. If the hotel there could accommodate us, we were going to stay there at least a second night. We had allowed a fortnight for the holiday and still had a day or two in hand, but, apart from that, there was nothing to stop us from putting in another week if we felt so inclined. Our return tickets to London from Glasgow were valid for a month, so no problem there, and I had money enough to cover any extra expenses and could get more in Glasgow if we needed it.

At last the climbing was over and The Way began to descend. I knew, however, that to get to Kinlochleven there was more climbing ahead of us and I was becoming more and more anxious about Hera's powers of endurance. She knew what I was thinking, for, when we stopped to admire the view we got of Buachaille Etive Mor, she said, 'Stop worrying, Comrie. Women are much tougher than men. We have to be.'

We passed the way to the ski-lift and came on to a well-surfaced road and a car park. We passed Blackrock Cottage and then, thankfully, we found that The Way took us downhill again and across the moor to the remote but more than welcome Kingshouse hotel. I enquired at once about the possibility of extending our booking and, to my great relief, this turned out to be possible.

The hotel and its pine trees were grandly situated under the protection — or the menace — of mighty Beinn a'Chrulaiste and all around were other mountains and the moors. Fortunately Hera was so greatly taken with the setting that she made no objections to my booking us in for an extra night and, although I knew she would never admit it, I am sure she was relieved to think that we were to take a whole day off from walking.

I had one other card up my sleeve, but I had to be wary about how and when I played it. To get to the Kingshouse hotel we had had to cross a main road and I knew from the guidebook that a bus route went along it to Fort William. It was my intention to insist, when the omens seemed favourable, that we should catch a bus and finish our journey that way. I thought of complaining of blisters on my feet, but the necessary evidence for this was lacking. I wondered whether I could fake a sprained ankle, but this would be inconvenient later if I had to cry off climbing Ben Nevis, a project on which she had set her heart.

In the event, I adopted neither subterfuge, but opted for yet another night at the hotel, pointing out to Hera that a stay of three nights entitled us to a rebate on the day-to-day terms charged, although whether this was the case I neither knew nor cared. Finally I put it to her bluntly that I had booked us for the third night as well as the second one and that she must please herself about what she wanted to do, but that I was determined to stay.

'We've covered sixty miles since we left Drymen,' I said. 'A good deal more, if you count the extra miles we covered when we lost our way in the mist. We've proved our point, don't you think?'

'I'm not sure about that,' she answered. 'I don't terribly care for your protective attitude. It isn't really protective, you know. It's mere self-assertion and male vanity. I detest this 'women and children first' nonsense. On a ship the sailors are the people to be considered. As for the Victorian ideal of the captain's either being the last to leave the vessel or even going down with it, I never heard such poppycock! The leader ought to be the principal survivor, not the inevitable casualty.'

'Why?'

'For obvious reasons, I should have thought. Where would the sheep be, if the shepherd died?'

'So what exactly are you getting at?'

'Go and get us more drinks and I'll tell you. You see,' she went on when I returned, 'you were very quick to hustle me away from that corpse. I won't blame you for that, except to say that it was high-handed and unnecessary.'

'You didn't *really* want to see a murdered man, particularly somebody we knew,' I said.

'But are you sure that it *was* somebody we knew? You only flashed your torch on him before you were grabbing me by the arm and dragging me back to that other room and then forcing me to get back to our road.'

'What is all this? Of course we had to get back on to our road. We had to get to the hotel.'

'I still think that, if you saw what you say you saw, we ought to go to the police. There might be all sorts of things for them to find out.'

'We've been into all this.'

'Look, when the mist came down and we lost our way, how far ahead of us were the other four?'

'If there still were four of them. The Minches might have left Todd and Carbridge by then. Everybody else had left them.'

'In any case, whether there were four of them or just the two men, they might have got to that turning we took long before the mist came down. Why should they have gone off the track? What made them leave The Way and go junketing away across country? It's too far-fetched to suppose that they were trying to take a short cut by the same route we had chosen. It doesn't make sense.'

'They may have heard about the ruins and wanted to take a look at them.' I knew this could not be true. Hera picked up the suggestion and threw it away.

'The ruins are not mentioned in the guidebook. Besides, Carbridge wanted to get to Fort William quickly. He wasn't any too pleased when Perth and the students spent that time at Inchcailloch on Loch Lomond and he dropped them altogether later on because they wanted to linger and collect bits of rocks and things. Why should he — or any of the others, for that matter — have wasted their time and energy going off the marked route?'

'You tell me,' I said.

'When you went charging down that dark passage you talk about, did you slip?'

'No, I fell over the body, as I told you. If you're thinking of blood, it coagulates pretty quickly unless the chap is a haemophiliac.'

'Why wouldn't you let me see him?'

'Oh, my dear girl, don't be morbid!'

'I might have been able to do something.'

'Don't talk so daft. He was dead, frozen, and as stiff as a board, I tell you.'

'I still think we ought to go to the police.'

'No. And that's flat. We hardly knew the chap and it's no business of ours what's happened to him. We've had all this out before. Heaven knows what sort of scandal we might get ourselves mixed up in, apart from the ghastly business of interviews with the police and being quizzed by reporters and having to appear in court at God knows what inconvenient time. They don't even hold inquests up here, I believe. It's straight into the rough stuff if the Procurator Fiscal thinks there's a case to answer, as in this instance there damn' well would be.'

'All right,' she said reluctantly. 'You've made your point, but I'm not going to say I'm happy about it. That poor man!'

'Probably only got what he asked for.'

'I didn't realise how callous you can be.'

'That's not callousness, it's only common sense. And now snap out of it.'

But, of course, neither of us could do that, and it was a silent and not exactly a compatible pair of love-birds who resumed their journey a couple of days later. However, encouraged by my unusually high-handed victory, I laid down the law again and, to my astonishment, this time she capitulated without a fight.

'Very well,' she said. 'Let's take to the main roads and do Ballachulish and on to Fort William, if we can pick up any transport, but heaven knows how the buses run in these parts.'

However, we were in luck. We had not been waiting at the roadside for more than ten minutes before a whacking great car with a man and a woman in it pulled up and the man put his head out. From the size of the vehicle and the fact that it had a left-hand drive, I guessed that the couple were from the States and this proved to be the case. Moreover, they were bound for Ballachulish, so we could not have been more lucky.

Needless to say, we did not mention the dead man, but they were greatly interested when they heard about The Way. The woman asked innumerable questions. I was on tenterhooks in case Hera should give away, after all, the secret of our visit to the ruins and the gruesome discovery I had made there, but she was discretion itself and as the car diminished the distance between Kingshouse and our destination, I became easier in my mind.

The couple were inclined to dismiss the magnificent Grampians as mere foothills compared with their own Rockies, but allowed that, compared with the mountains of Switzerland and Austria, those in the Highlands had 'atmosphere'. In any case, whatever the views of the couple and however subversive they were, neither Hera nor I was prepared to quarrel with them, for we were much too grateful for the lift to be in any mood to argue with the kindly and voluble Americans. It was not until almost the end of the journey that we discovered that they were really bound for Oban and had come miles out of their way for our sakes. After we had crossed the bridge at Ballachulish, they took us all the way to Fort William.

'Think nothing of it,' the driver said. 'My wife is wild to see Glen Coe where the massacre took place, so we were bound for Ballachulish anyhow. All we need to do is go back-along and then pick up our route south. At Oban I aim to take pictures and then cross the only bridge over the Atlantic. Boy! Will that be something to tell the folks back home!' He was referring to the bridge which connects the mainland to the little island of

Seil on the road from Oban to Easdale. I remembered it well from the coach tour with my parents, for I had been young enough to believe that the coach really *was* going to cross to America.

The youth hostel at Fort William was about three miles from the town shops, but it was marvellously well situated, as I knew, for the climb up Ben Nevis. It was a Grade One hostel, had one hundred and twenty-eight beds, cooking facilities and a shop, but meals were not provided, so we bought our own food from the hostel store. When we went into the kitchen to cook it, who should be there but Rhoda and Tansy. They had put up at a hotel for three nights and then come on to the hostel. They and we were the only people at the hostel when we arrived. The weather was fine and the other hostellers either had not yet arrived or were out enjoying themselves. I became more and more grateful to the kindly Americans for the welcome lift they had given us from Kingshouse to Fort William, for, if we climbed Ben Nevis on the morrow, it meant at least a seven-hour stint and some rough going, even by the easiest ascent. To have cut out the long miles and overnight stop if we had completed the walk was a marvellous bonus. We crossed the bridge opposite the hostel and looked around us. It was pleasant in the glen, but I had climbed Ben Nevis once before, and I knew that conditions could be very different when we reached the summit. Hera was all eagerness and anticipation, so I warned her that the way up the great (and, to my mind, very ugly) mountain was not only arduous in places, but could be extremely dull.

'But think of the view from the summit!' she said.

'Well enough, so long as the weather holds and the Ben isn't capped by cloud.'

'It won't be. We haven't come all this way for nothing. If it's no good tomorrow, we can wait a day, can't we?'

'We're only booked in for tonight and this is a very popular hostel,' I pointed out.

'Then we'll go to a hotel. Why not?'

But she was not to climb Ben Nevis on that holiday, for, because of the most startling and utterly unforeseen circumstance, we were out of that hostel as soon as next morning's breakfast was over. We lost no time in making for the railway station and in taking the train for Glasgow. We were fleeing, as it were, from a disembodied spirit and terrified, so far as I myself was concerned, not for my life, but for my reason. At about seven o'clock that evening when, taking advantage of the fact that only a few hostellers had drifted in, Hera and I had cooked and eaten our simple supper rather earlier than we really wanted it, a lot of hostellers, all chatting and laughing, came in. Among the crowd were four people we knew. The next moment Hera and I were hailed by Carbridge, Todd and the Minches, all very much alive, although tired, they said, from their climb. To clinch matters, we were joined an hour later by Perth and the students. They had climbed with the others, but had stayed longer on the mountain to add little bits of lava and granite to the collection they had already made at Inchcailloch and along The Way and had despatched to London to avoid having to tote so much heavy material on the rest of their march.

When Carbridge and his companions came in, I heard Hera give a peculiar little cry. As for me, I was so flabbergasted that I could feel my head swimming and I suppose I came as near to fainting as I have ever been in my life. However, it was Carbridge all right and as full of effervescence and bonhomie as ever. He appeared to have forgotten our dispute and my high-handed action at Crianlarich, and soon the 'old boy, old boy' stuff began again, and the advice to Hera: 'My tip, fair one, is to avoid that climb unless you go up by pony.'

Before the footweary but triumphant quartet — Jane's feet must have responded to my treatment — had gone to the kitchen quarters to prepare something which would restore their wasted tissues, Hera dragged me outside and on to the bridge over the River Nevis again.

'You told me he was *dead!* You said you *fell over him!* You said he had been *murdered!* You said he had a *knife* in his back! You said he was *stone-cold and stiff!*' she babbled. Well, shock has different effects on different people. Now that I had recovered a little, the shock of seeing him had made me reckless.

'So you believed all that guff,' I said. 'Poor old you!'

She smacked my face and, as I suppose I was really somewhat hysterical at the time, this summary treatment had its usual result. I apologised and assured her that I had been certain it was the body of Carbridge that I had seen. I tried to take her hand. She shook me off, turned aside and began to cry.

'For heaven's sake, stop it!' I said. 'When they've had their meal, we've got to face that lot again.' We did. There was much euphoria. There was triumph that they had walked The Way and much exhibiting of souvenirs they had bought in Fort William. Todd, said Carbridge, had been the favourite of the ladies. Tansy and Patsy had both bought him presents.

When they had all turned in for the night, I said, 'Darling, I *did* fall over him, I *did* see him. I *did* touch him. I could have sworn it was he. I spoke out of turn just now, I know I did, but please don't hold it against me. I've had the most awful shock. You can't imagine what it was like when that lot walked in. And then, when you turned on me — '

'I didn't turn on you. Don't you think I had a shock, too, after all you'd said?'

'Yes, of course, but (and, please, I am not intending to start an argument) I do think my shock must have been more severe than yours.'

'So you were telling me the truth? — or, at any rate, you thought you were.'

'Darling, I swear I was!'

'Then,' she said, with a complete return to her usual forthrightness, 'we'll go home first thing tomorrow and when we get back to London you'd better see a psychiatrist. I'm not going to father my children on a man who sees a corpse where no corpse is. All that nonsense about falling over it in a dark passage!'

'There *was* a corpse all right,' I said, 'but I made a mistake about whose corpse it was. I suppose I was badly rattled, and you must admit that Carbridge is a very ordinary-looking bloke. So far as his clothes are concerned.'

'Well, I'm glad now that you wouldn't let me go to the police. Nice fools we should have looked if we had reported finding a dead man who, a day or two later, was able to climb Ben Nevis and eat a hearty supper afterwards.'

'Look, I made a mistake. Do I have to keep on spelling it out?'

'I've looked a lot of times at the map since we started out. There's no castle marked.'

'It wasn't a castle, I tell you. It was only a ruin and probably wasn't important even in its heyday.'

'Can you remember what the place looked like?'

'I think so. Why? If we're not going to the police, I shan't need to describe it to anybody.'

'Just as well, perhaps.'

'Could *you* describe it?'

'No, of course I couldn't, but I would be willing to agree to your description if it ever came to the point. A thick mist, like the one we ran into, sends my wits wool-gathering. I never could find my way in a fog.'

I looked suspiciously at her.

'Are you trying to tell me something?' I asked.

'Yes,' she said, with an emphasis I could not account for at the time. 'I want you to see a psychiatrist or a doctor, or an eye specialist, or even all three, as soon as we get back to London.'

'I'll be shot if I do!' I said hotly. 'What are you getting at, for God's sake?'

She smiled in a cat-like way and repeated that I needed my head, my blood pressure and my eyes tested. I could have struck her to the ground. Instead, I attempted a verbal attack.

'You're becoming senile,' I said. I thought the ungentlemanly shaft would hurt her. It did not. She still smiled.

'Yes, but I wear well,' she said, 'which is more than you do. When I was your age, at least I didn't see things which weren't there.'

She was four years older than I was, a fact I had always deplored.

'If you are going to make nasty cracks about what I saw or didn't see, I shall marry Jane Minch,' I said.

She laughed. 'The children will look like plover's eggs,' she said. 'Those freckles! Oh, my God!'

# 6

## *A Visit to a Psychiatrist*

We were lucky with the train from Glasgow, where we spent the night. The run from there to Euston passed without incident and, except that I was aware that she was keeping an eye on me, I might have thought that Hera had forgotten all about what had happened. The only spoken reference she made to our excursion in the mist was in the form of a quotation from a nostalgic poem by W. J. Turner. We were reminiscing about our walk along The Way, but steering well clear of our visit to the ruins, when she said, looking at me in a commiserating sort of way which was rather galling:

> ' "I dimly heard the master's voice
> And boys far-off at play,
> Chimborazo, Cotopaxi
> Had stolen me away." '

'I am not a thirteen-year-old schoolboy, and what I saw and touched had nothing to do with the mountains of Ecuador,' I said, 'still less with the Grampians of Scotland.'

'Knows his geography, too!' she said, with the simulated admiration she might have extended to a bright child of five. I grinned, determined not to allow her to see that she had irritated me.

'If you let out a crack like that when we're married, I'll clout you,' I said.

'Another infantile reaction,' she retorted, so, as usual, she had the last word. We had dinner in Soho, then I took her by taxi to her flat and walked back to my own. I had nothing but my rucksack to carry. She had invited me in, but I knew that, if

I accepted the invitation, we should either quarrel or make love, or perhaps the one would follow the other, and who knew in which order?

'You're angry with me,' she said, when I would not go in.

'No,' I said. 'Sometimes I'd like to murder you, but I'm never angry with you.'

'Sometimes? Never? Do those come under the heading of lies, damned lies, or statistics? And perhaps we had better not mention murder for a bit. I might begin to think you are obsessed by it.'

So, like the chap in *A Shropshire Lad*, I walked home alone 'amidst the moonlight pale', and while I walked and long after I had let myself into my flat and had gone to bed, I turned over in my mind all that had happened since I had been in London the last time. It did not make for comforting thoughts. I reviewed everything that I remembered about the mist, the realisation that we had lost our way, the unexpected discovery of the stone wall, its entrance arch, the glassless window through which we had climbed and my subsequent discovery of the body. It was of no use to tell myself that only some of this had happened. Either all of it, or none of it, I told myself, had fallen within my experience. I was worried and fearful.

'Well, how did your holiday go?' asked my partner when I turned up at our offices a couple of days later. 'You're back early, aren't you? Anything go wrong?'

'Sandy,' I said, 'I am going to describe to you all the objects which I imagine I can see in this room and you will check with me whether I am really seeing them or not. Or – no!' I went on. 'I might only *think* you were agreeing with me. In fact, for all I know, you may not be here at all, and neither may I, come to that. There's no proof, is there?'

He looked at me with eyes which were both sceptical and concerned.

'I suppose you didn't roll down a mountain and hit your head while you were in Scotland, did you?' he asked.

'No, of course not. At least – well, no.'

'Then what's all this about?'

So I told him everything. After all, we had been at school and college together and there had always been a strong bond between us, and I hoped I could at least trust him not to laugh at me.

'All I can say,' he said, when he had told the girl in the outer office to fob off all callers, whether personal or by telephone, until he gave the all clear, 'is that you only *thought* the fellow was dead. He must have come back to consciousness a bit later on, rejoined his party and gone on to Fort William, while you were lazing the time away at the Kingshouse hotel.'

'I don't think that's possible. I *know* there was a corpse. Hera thinks I ought to see a psychiatrist. She's hedging about our marriage, I'm afraid.'

'Well, obviously the poor girl doesn't fancy yoking herself with a fellow for whom the wagon may come trundling round at any minute.'

'It's not funny, Sandy. I shone my torch on the chap as well as touching him, you see. Either I'm potty or something very strange has happened.'

'Well, look, to ease your mind, why don't you fall in with Hera's idea? She's been phoning me. Why don't you consult a psychiatrist? They're not all cranks, you know.'

'She only mentioned it once. I don't think she was all that serious. Surely she couldn't have been. I had no idea, though, that she had been talking to you. What else did she say?'

'Look, if she's got any doubts in her mind, the best thing is to set them at rest as soon as you can.'

'I don't know any psychiatrists.'

'That is where I have the advantage of you. I know the best one in the country. She isn't a quack; she won't feed you a lot of hot air all ballooned up in the jargon some of these people use, and she's fully qualified in medicine as well as in psychiatry.'

'She?'

'Dame Beatrice Adela Lestrange Bradley. You'll like her. I'll ring up and make the appointment, if you like. She only takes cases which interest her, and I think she'll fall for yours.

Besides, we've got her granddaughter on our list.'

'We have?'

'Sally Lestrange, the occasional novelist and a ghostwriter for the non-literary bods who have a life story to tell. Dame Beatrice will sort you out.'

'Why should you think so? You're as bad as Hera. You both think I'm bats just because I identified a dead body wrongly.'

'I don't think that's the whole story, Comrie, old chap. Hera doesn't think so, either. Tell me, are you suffering from some sort of frustration?'

'How do you mean?'

'You've slept with Hera more than once. She told me so. She says she thinks she was too hard on you when she wouldn't let you book a double room at the hotels in Scotland. She said it was expecting too much of a hot-blooded he-man — '

'The last thing I am, and the last thing she thinks about me. Good Lord, I can exercise self-restraint when I've got to! It was all part of her plan. It was the whole object of the holiday. What do you think I am? — the lineal descendant of thousands of ever-copulating rabbits?'

'I'm only telling you what Hera said about the strain she put upon you during that holiday. As you suspected, she has already told me the whole story. It's not as though *she* saw that dead body — '

'Only because I took care she didn't. One doesn't introduce sensitive girls to itinerant corpses.'

'She also says she can't remember any castle.'

'There wasn't any bloody castle! She's the one who needs a psychiatrist, not I. Anyway, it was a fort. I suppose she doesn't remember the mist and our losing our way in it.'

'Oh, yes, she admits to the mist. She said that, because of it, and because you tried to take a short cut, you both wandered off your route, but she says you had hit your head pretty badly and that most of your story is sheer fantasy. She's very worried about you.'

'Perhaps she'd like to break the engagement,' I said. 'I felt there was a hint of it in the air.'

'I think she might consider that course very seriously. What about you?'

I thought of a freckled child I had held in my arms, and did not answer.

I knew Dame Beatrice's name, of course, in the way one knows the name of most celebrities, but I had never thought that one day I should be asking for a consultation. An assured voice answered the telephone.

'Dame Beatrice Lestrange Bradley?' I asked hopefully, for the voice inspired confidence.

'Who is speaking?' I gave my name and asked whether Dame Beatrice would see me. I was asked my business.

'I'd like to become a patient,' I said.

'She takes very few cases nowadays. What's the trouble? You can tell me. I'm her secretary.'

'I've recently come back from walking some of the West Highland Way, and I've had a very disturbing experience.'

'All right. Hold the line.' I waited, but not for long. When she contacted me again, she said, 'What kind of experience?'

'I stumbled over the dead body of a man I thought I knew. This was somewhere on Rannoch Moor, but he turned up hale and hearty at Fort William.'

'Sounds promising. Well, I've been told to use my own discretion, so I think you had better come along. Thursday, as near eleven in the morning as you can manage, would be the most suitable time and day.'

I say I knew Dame Beatrice's name, but I was not prepared for her appearance and still less was I prepared for her beautiful voice. She would have become, I thought, a singer of great repute had she chosen the concert hall instead of medicine and psychiatry. In appearance she was small and thin, dressed like a macaw, and had brilliant black eyes. She would never have 'made it' in opera. I cannot think of any role she could fill.

'Now,' she said, when the tall secretary had left us, 'there is plenty of time before lunch. Do you care to walk round the garden and look at the stables, or shall we "get down to the nitty-gritty", as I believe you modern young people express it?'

'I'm feeling a bit embarrassed and very nervous,' I said.

'Very useful and, of course, quite natural. Sit down again.'

'Not a couch?' I asked, feeling rather like a man jesting with the dentist or on the morning of his execution.

'We shall see. State your case.'

I do not know whether it was the eyes, the pursed-up little mouth or the beautiful voice which convinced me from the very outset of the interview that my mind was going to be set at rest, but so it proved. She told me to take my time and that is what I did. When she heard all that I could tell her, she said, 'A pity you and your fiancée do not read the Scottish newspapers. Have no fear for your reason, my dear Mr Melrose. You *did* find a corpse. The only thing is that you did not manage to identify it correctly.'

'There *was* a dead man in those ruins?'

'Of course there was a dead man.' I thought she looked at me in an appraising way. 'Ring the bell twice.'

I did this and it was answered by the secretary. I suppose she had been briefed beforehand, for she was carrying some newspapers which, without being instructed to do so, she handed to me as I resumed my seat opposite Dame Beatrice. It occurred to me that Sandy had been on the telephone before I arrived.

'Another heart is set at rest, I opine,' said the secretary.

'Mr Melrose is fortunate that you read your country's press, Laura,' said Dame Beatrice. 'Again take your time, Mr Melrose. You will find those journalistic outpourings both heartening and of interest.'

I read avidly. The body had been identified as that of an ex-convict called McConachie, and the conclusion seemed to be that he had been tracked down, after an attempted strangulation, and stabbed to death by one of his acquaintances whom he had double-crossed when it came to the division of the spoils. The police had received a tip-off (not from Hera, I hoped), had visited the area and had found the body. Identification was no problem. The man's photograph and fingerprints were on record and the police were in no doubt as to his identity and that of the murderer.

My relief, intense though it was, was accompanied by a sense of anti-climax. Was it for this sordid and uninspiring solution that I had sacrificed sleep and my peace of mind, had almost quarrelled with Hera and wrecked any pleasure I might have had in recollecting my holiday? Thoughts of the holiday, however, emboldened me, over lunch, to put a question to Dame Beatrice.

'I told you what was the object of the exercise,' I said. 'Why Hera and I took the holiday?'

'To test whether you and your fiancée were sufficiently compatible in temperament to risk taking one another in marriage, I think you said.'

'Yes. Well, if I may ask such a question, what do *you* think, now that you've heard the whole story?'

'Ask Laura. She can usually read my mind.'

'Some chicken, some neck!' said Laura obscurely, but I knew what she meant. I, too, found Dame Beatrice formidable. 'All right, then.' Laura said. 'If it were up to me, I'm bound to say I think you're batting on a sticky wicket. Your young woman wears the trousers at present. That's all right during the period of wooing, but I'm not sure it would work in married life. You would find yourself the toad under the harrow.'

'I've no particular wish to be top dog,' I said, feeling nettled by her summing-up.

'No, but marriage should be an equal partnership. Why wouldn't you let her see the body?'

'Oh, dash it all! One doesn't deliberately give a girl a shock of that kind!'

'The shock might have been less for her than it was for you,' said Dame Beatrice. 'Tell me — had you anything personal against this man whose corpse you thought it was?'

'He irritated me, just as he irritated everyone else. There was another chap whom I was also anxious to keep my eye on, this fellow named Todd. I mentioned him when I was telling you about the holiday.'

'Yes, but you never thought it was Todd's body you found?'

'No. I was certain I'd found Carbridge, but, of course, I didn't exactly linger beside the corpse. All I wanted was to get Hera away from the place as soon as ever I could. I just grabbed her and dragged her out, although it was raining buckets when we got on to the moor.'

'Yes, what about this place? Do you retain a vivid picture of it? These ruins, do you recall them clearly?'

'Well, no, I wouldn't call it a vivid picture. I had hit my head rather hard, if you see what I mean. The ruins seemed as full of mist as the moor outside. My recollection of them is hazy.'

'But you remember coming to a wall, ducking under an archway and climbing into the ruins through an embrasure?'

'Well, it seems a bit nebulous now, but, yes, I'm sure I remember all that. Well, no, perhaps I dreamt that part of it. I'm sure Hera believes I dreamt the whole thing, including finding the body.'

'Not surprising,' said Laura, 'when the same body turned up hale and hearty at Fort William. Enough to cause any right-minded girl to have doubts. Still, you'll be able to reassure her now. Keep the papers and show them to her. They ought to convince her that at least there was a corpse and that you found it.'

'I wish I could convince her that there was a building, too. She seems to doubt the whole story. The only bit she really agrees with is that we lost our way in the mist.'

'Yes,' said Dame Beatrice. 'What about the dark passage?'

'I'm sure about that,' I replied.

The two women looked at one another. Then Dame Beatrice said, 'There is something you are keeping to yourself. Had you not better tell me what it is?'

'No, there's nothing,' I said. I could feel her brilliant eyes probing my brain. 'Unless you mean the row I had with Todd at Crianlarich, but it was only a verbal exchange. Fisticuffs did not come into it.'

'It was not Mr Todd's body you mistook, you see. Interesting, but are you sure about that?' I said I was perfectly certain, so she said, 'Well, Mr Melrose, I do not think you need psychiatry, but we shall see how matters develop. We must wait upon events.'

'I hope there won't be any, so far as this business is concerned,' I said. 'Thank you very much for the papers.'

'Sit down again,' said Dame Beatrice, for I had risen to go. 'Tell me more about this set-to you had with Mr Todd.'

'Oh, it was nothing,' I said. 'As a matter of fact, he apologised.'

'For what?'

'For trying to persuade Hera to opt out of the youth hostel and go to the hotel for the night, so I tackled him and sorted him out. "Honestly, I had no idea she was engaged to you," he said. "When I met you two at the airport hotel, I just thought it was a holiday pick-up and that you'd got together because you found you were both going to walk The Way. After all, she doesn't wear a keep-off-the-grass ring, does she?" I told him the engagement hadn't been announced, but that there was a ring in her possession. He apologised again and said he hoped no hard feelings. It was a genuine misunderstanding, he said. Well, that was the end of it because, of course, we didn't run into him again until we got to Fort William.'

I showed Sandy the newspapers and I got to our office next day.

'So the visit was a good idea,' he said.

'Yes and no.'

'How do you mean? You said you fell over a corpse and there *was* a corpse.'

'Yes,' I said, 'one corpse, no stone walls, apparently. The police found the corpse on the moor, the papers say. They don't mention a building.'

'Plenty of rocks about. You mistook some outcrop or other for a stone wall. Easy mistake to make in a thick mist after you'd bashed your head. Possibly, though, the police want to keep the actual location secret. Have you shown Hera the newspapers?'

'Not yet. I'm seeing her tonight.'

'Well,' said Sandy, giving me a very straight glance, 'take the strong, manly course and rub her disbelieving little nose in the reports. She's been more than a bit uppish about you and that corpse, you know.'

'You mean she said more to you than she has to me?'

'More than likely. She's had me on the phone a couple of times and rather spread herself. Seems to think you're the kind of sensitive plant that dreams dreams and sees visions. These newspapers ought to provide her with a healthier outlook.'

'But what about the archway and the window where we climbed in? Apparently they don't exist. All the papers say is that the police found the body on Rannoch Moor. I've told you that already.'

'And I've reminded you of that knock on the head. That and the mist confused you, that's all.'

'I swear there was a dark passage.'

'Forget it. It's all over and done with now.'

But I could not forget it, for it brought back memories of an experience I had had in my childhood and had pushed to the back of my mind because it frightened me. I was eight years old at the time and I told my father that burglars had killed our dog and broken in. It happened two days later. Now, after twenty years, it all came back to me, and a very uncomfortable memory it was!

I began to regret that I had kept back from Dame Beatrice a full account of what had happened at Crianlarich. However, it seemed rather late in the day to worry about that, particularly as the body had not been that of Carbridge. I could not face the prospect of going back to the Stone House and confessing that I had not told the whole truth about my murderous attack on Carbridge. In the end, I consulted Sandy.

'It can't make any difference, can it?' I said.

'I shouldn't think so. She probably guessed you were hiding something, anyway. She said you didn't need psychiatry, didn't she?'

'Yes, but that was because I hadn't been "seeing things". There was a corpse and the chap had been murdered.'

'But you thought it was Carbridge. That sounds to me like the promptings of a guilty conscience.'

'I only had an electric torch and that passage was as black as Erebus.'

'All the same, it was a strange mistake for you to make. It seems you must have some kind of fixation regarding the chap.'

'I find him excessively irritating, that's all.'

'So irritating that you wish he were dead?'

'No, of course not. Once I'd got over the first shock when he walked into the hostel at Fort William, I was enormously pleased and relieved to know that he was safe and well, particularly as it was obvious he bore me no malice whatever.'

'These "bear no malice" blokes are a funny bunch. I suppose most of them profess and call themselves Christians, but, you know, Comrie, nobody really forgives a person who has made him look a nithing.'

'A what?'

'A nithing. It's an Anglo-Saxon word, I think, meaning a thing of no account, a No Thing, a coward, somebody who can be disregarded, a fellow who cuts no ice. Nobody ever sees himself thus. Men resent anything and everything which questions their virility, their attraction for the opposite sex, their physical courage and their sense of humour, particularly the last-named. You've made an enemy and I wouldn't despise him if I were you. He'll get back at you some day.'

'You make my flesh creep,' I said. He laughed, but I knew he spoke seriously. Besides, there was something in what he said. I had expressed my opinion of Carbridge in Crianlarich and yet he had the insolence to come back at me again at Fort William with his 'fair one' greeting to Hera. It had been a challenge and I had not known how to meet it. Carbridge had called my bluff and got away with it. The strange thing was that I no longer cared. I wondered whether this meant that I had cooled off towards Hera, or whether the relief of knowing that the silly fellow was alive was so great that, like some tremendous tide, it had washed all my animosity away.

# 7

# *A Reunion*

To say that I was surprised when Hera and I received the invitation is to put it more than mildly. That we accepted it seems, with hindsight, to have been the mistake of a lifetime. It came three weeks before the late August Bank Holiday and was for a reunion of those of us who had met on The Way, to be held the Saturday in that weekend. Had it come from Carbridge or Todd, I feel sure we would have turned it down, but it came from the students and was signed by all four of them, Lucius Trickett, Coral Platt, Freddie Brown and Patsy Carlow.

'We must go,' said Hera decisively. Although she had mellowed considerably towards me after she had read the Scottish newspapers, she still vigorously asserted herself.

'We shall be bored rigid,' I said.

'Nonsense. Student parties are always fun and I expect they have gone to no end of trouble to organise this one. We can't let them down. They will be giving up a lot of their summer vacation to lay on the festivities and goodness knows how much they'll have to scrimp up out of their grants to pay for a party.'

'We'd better take a couple of bottles along to help out, in that case, and let them know we're bringing something,' I said.

'You will accept, then? Oh, good! I'll send the answer in both our names, if you like. I know how you procrastinate over everything except business letters. I suppose they got our addresses from the telephone book.'

'Or from the Scottish Youth Hostel registers while they were up there. All right, you answer for both of us and I'll note down the date in my diary and see about the drinks.'

'I wonder what we'll be expected to wear?'

'Casuals, of course.'

The function was to be held in one of the polytechnic's halls of residence, a large house in Bloomsbury. Hera thought we might spend the afternoon at the British Museum and go on to the party from there. It would make for conversation, she said, if the going was sticky at first.

'They are such serious children, that lot,' she explained. 'I wonder whether anybody besides The Way people will be there?'

'Probably more of the poly students in order to make things go, but no doubt Carbridge can do that on his own — at least, he'll think so. I expect he'll assume charge of the whole proceedings unless the party turns out to be a student version of *Top of the Pops* with time out for potato crisps, salted peanuts, little sausages on sticks, mousetrap cheese, sherry which, in the classic phrase, would burn the shell off an egg, and a barrel of beer for the boys,' I said. 'How I do hate drinking beer at four in the afternoon!'

'What's wrong with *Top of the Pops*?'

'Nothing, if you like that kind of thing. I always switch off the set, because I can't stick these moronic atavisms.'

'Don't be so toffee-nosed.'

'Just as you say. I'll go, but I don't expect to enjoy myself, that is all I intended to convey.'

'You'll love it when you get there.'

'So they always told me as a child when I jibbed at going to other children's Christmas and birthday parties.'

'Well, didn't you enjoy yourself?'

'No.' Emboldened by my uncompromising use of this splendid negative, I added, 'And you need not think you are going to drag me to the Brit. Mus., either. I shall spend the day enjoying myself and then I shall don jeans and a Wild West shirt for the revels.'

'And find that the other men have turned up in immaculate flannels. I shall wear a frock,' she said.

However, her slinky little dress, which I had so admired, looked out-of-place against the slacks, jeans and, in the case of the student Patsy Carlow — who, with Lucius Trickett, was organising the dancing — Turkish trousers, gold lamé chest-protectors in the shape of little targets, and a sort of Isadora Duncan turban.

The Minches wore kilts of tartan woven in a bold mixture of red and white which, as I discovered later, they were entitled to wear, his with a sporran, hers without, and both sporting vast safety-pins to keep the body and soul of the garment in decent contiguity. Todd had compromised by wearing grey flannels and a soft silk shirt, attire in which he looked both elegant and comfortable. I envied him and wished I had thought of the same clothing for myself.

The only member of the student party who had not turned up was Perth, but that was understandable as his home was in Glasgow, so it would have been expecting rather much of him to travel to London for an occasion which was of only a few hours' duration. What *did* astonish me was the absence of Carbridge. Far from being the life and soul of the party, he was not in attendance at all.

The insurance-office women, Rhoda and Tansy, were present though, and had played safe by wearing light summer dresses bought (or so Hera informed me) at Marks and Sparks. I think she regretted her slinky little number and would gladly have exchanged outfits with Tansy, who was much about her size.

The music, if one calls it that — I suppose some people do — was provided by a group of young people whom I took to be fellow-students of Perth's lot, since every so often they abandoned guitars, a trumpet, a saxophone, a trombone, the piano, a double bass and the detonation of drums and the clash of cymbals in favour of turning on a gramophone and joining in the dancing.

Our other two students, Freddie and Coral, rushed in with dishes of sizzling chipolata sausages or tin trays of hamburgers, and the food was seized on greedily by the dancers and consumed at lightning speed, to be followed, time after time, by fresh consignments of what seemed a never-ending, inexhaustible supply. There was plenty of beer and bottles of fizz to drink.

Hera, Todd and I were given the gin and tonics I had brought.

What with the fact that the size of the room was not over-adequate for its purpose — because of the area taken up by the piano, the musicians, a table for the gramophone and records, and the amount of space required by each dancer and the necessity for these to keep a clear passage for the everlasting relays of food, not to mention three long trestle tables bearing mugs, tumblers and bottles — I soon grew tired of the din, the heat, the glistening sweaty faces of the males and the screaming voices of females determined to converse, whatever odds were stacked against their being heard, and I began to feel the necessity for solitude, peace and a quiet cigarette. Hera spotted me sneaking towards the door.

'And where do you think *you're* going?' she demanded.

'Out for a quiet puff or two, that's all.'

'You're not trying to "steal away home" like the singer of the negro spiritual?'

'Of course not. I wouldn't go without telling you.'

'That's all right, then. Are you hating all this?'

'No, no. I like to see young people happy.'

I slipped out and walked down a long, broad corridor. It was not the way by which we had been taken to what I supposed was the common-room, but the house was a large one and the room had three doors. The corridor was occupied by a bloke near the further end. He was seated behind a small table near a glass-fronted telephone cabinet, reading one newspaper and eating fish and chips out of another.

'Is there anywhere I can go to have a quiet smoke?' I asked him. 'I've got a bit of a headache with all the row in there.'

'Why, yes, sir. Go along a bit further and on your left you'll find a passage. There's a switch on the right as you goes in. Oh, Lor', though! You'll have to feel your way, I'm afraid, sir. I'd clean forgot. I recollects now as some clever bugger have removed the electric lightbulb. Wanted it for his own room, I suppose. Some of 'em comes in during the vacations to get on with a bit of college work, you see. I better get around to replacing it. But you'll find your way all right and the door is straight in front of you.'

It dawned on me that he thought my modest desire for a quiet smoke meant that I really needed the Gents, but I decided that at any rate I could stand outside its door and have my puff, so I thanked him and walked on, as he had directed.

That is to say, I *began* to walk on as he had directed, but in the little passage — dark as the one in Scotland — I stumbled over a body.

They talk of people who feel they are living in a nightmare. That is not a novelist's exaggerated way of expressing the extreme of discomfort and terror. I can vouch for its literal truth. Before I struck a match to look at what was on the floor of that dark passage, I questioned whether I was not indeed in the throes of a nightmare and I wondered how soon I could wake myself out of it. I could feel every nerve in my body clicking with electric sparks. It *must* be a nightmare, I thought.

But, of course, it was no nightmare, but a stark and dreadful reality. I rallied with what has become known as the courage of despair, pulled myself together and struck the match. When it scorched my fingers, I dropped it and went back to the man in the broad, well-lit corridor. I don't know what I looked like, but he stood up, came out from behind his table, took my arm and said in a voice of deep concern, 'Are you all right, sir?'

'Yes — no — yes. Look, could you come with me a minute? There's a — there's a dead man in that passage.'

'You sit yourself down in my chair, sir, while I fetches one of the other gentlemen,' he said.

'Good Lord! He thinks I'm mad,' I said aloud.

'There, there! Just you take it easy,' he said soothingly. He almost galloped along the corridor towards the room where the party was being held. I put my elbows on the table and held my head in my hands. Coral and Freddie, who were serving the food, came up with loaded trays and stopped in front of me.

'Hullo, are you all right? Where's Bull gone?' asked the youth. I looked up and pointed towards the end of the corridor.

'You'd better wait here,' I said. 'Something has happened.'

'Oh, well,' said Coral, putting her tray down on the table, 'a chance to have a bite ourselves. Been so busy feeding the five thousand that we haven't had a look in on the bakemeats so far. Have a nosebag yourself. You look as though you could do with it.'

I could no more have done as she suggested than I could have partaken of the contents of a cannibal's stewpot, but just then the door of the common-room opened and the caretaker came back with Lucius Trickett. The students with the trays picked them up and departed to render service.

'This is the gentleman, Mr Trickett, sir,' said the caretaker.

'Oh, I say, you're Melrose,' said Trickett. 'Awfully glad you could come. Anything up?' To have attended the party was the last thing I was glad about, but I didn't say so. He went on: 'You're the chap who totes that awfully pretty woman around, aren't you? You know — Miss Camden, you know. She is probably wondering where you have got to. I say! You do look a bit peculiar. I'll call a doctor, shall I?'

'Call the police. There's a dead man in the passage,' I said.

They both looked at me with deep concern. Bull took the student aside.

'I think we had better take a look, just to humour him, sir,' I heard him say. 'Hang on a minute. I've got an electric torch in my den.' He went off to get it and Trickett seated himself on the table.

'Are you sloshed?' he asked. I shook my head.

'I wish I were,' I said. 'What's more, I could do with a double brandy right now. This is the second time this has happened to me.'

'Double vision, old man. All doubles, if you see what I mean.'

Bull came back with a torch and an electric bulb.

'You'll taller than me, sir, so won't need the step-ladder,' he said, handing Trickett the bulb. 'I'd have replaced this here before now, but for the bother of fetching the ladder.' They walked towards the end of the corridor. I got up from my chair and caught up with them, an action which I don't think either appreciated very much, for Bull said nervously, 'Now don't you fret, sir. Just leave everything to us. We'll soon fix up a light and then you'll see as everything is all right.'

But, of course, nothing was all right except the calm behaviour of Trickett. The electric light was only about a third of
the way down the passage, so, helped by the beam of Bull's
torch, Trickett was able to reach up and fix the bulb before we
came to the body. When he saw it he said, 'Well, well! Yes, Bull,
you had certainly better call the police.' He took me by the
sleeve. 'Come up to my room, Mr Melrose, and I'll rustle you up
a drink. You won't want to go back to the party.'

We went up some stairs, I remember, and he took me into his
study-bedroom. The drink was only vermouth, but it did something for me. I sat in his only chair while he settled himself on
the bed and, when I had swallowed the contents of the glass, I
told him all about my experience in the ruins on Rannoch
Moor.

'Oh, well,' he said comfortingly, 'it's not all that unusual for
people to see things before they happen. Time is only relative,
after all.'

'But the chap in Scotland was a real chap. I didn't see a
ghost. I just identified him wrongly, that's all. The really odd
thing — well, this chap in the passage *is* Carbridge.'

'Yes. It looks as though he turned up after all.'

'After all?'

'Yes. He answered the invitation with tremendous enthusiasm,
so I quite expected him to come bouncing along and I was most
surprised when he didn't show up.'

'Well, he's shown up now all right.'

'Yes,' said Trickett, gloomy for the first time, 'you're right
there. I don't know what the warden is going to say. He wasn't
a bit keen to grant me permission to hold the party here out of
term-time and, if it hadn't been a reunion for the Scottish ad-
venture people, he would have turned me down flat. He told me
so.' He looked at me sadly, but without animosity. 'You couldn't
be a sort of Ancient Mariner, could you?' he asked.

'I haven't killed the albatross or anything or anybody else.
I've just got myself caught up in something nightmarish,' I
answered; but the reference to the Ancient Mariner brought

my previous bad dreams rushing back at me like a flock of vampire bats.

Before I could say any more, Bull knocked on the door to tell us that the police had arrived. Would we please come down? We went down. A policeman was standing by the door behind which the party was held and two others, an inspector and a sergeant, both in uniform, were waiting at the foot of the stairs.

'Which of you gentlemen found the body?'

'I did,' I said.

'Gentleman was on his way to the bog,' said Bull helpfully.

'Well, it looks like a case for the CID,' said the inspector.

'Did you think it was a hoax, then?' asked Trickett sharply.

'We never know, with students.' The sergeant took down our names and addresses and the inspector sent us to join the rest of the party. Everybody realised that something was up. All the noise had died down, the orchestra had laid aside their instruments and the only sound except for low-toned conversation was made by the pianist, who was strumming very softly some plaintive tunes such as 'Swanee River' and 'Poor Old Joe'. I suppose he thought modern jazz would be out of place.

We all sat around on the floor, for only the orchestra had chairs. Hera sat beside me.

'So it was you who started all this,' she murmured, under cover of 'Massa's in de cold, cold ground'.

'Who else? Just my abominable luck. Don't dwell on it. I couldn't help it, could I?' I said.

'So said the child who swatted the fly on grandpa's head and caused the poor old man to end up in a lunatic asylum,' she said; and she certainly was not meaning to be funny. 'Tell me what has happened,' she demanded.

'I'd rather you heard it from the police,' I said. 'You would hardly believe it if *I* told you.'

'The police? You don't mean — you *can't* mean — ?'

'Yes,' I said, 'that's what I mean. Carbridge came to the party after all, in a manner of speaking.'

# 8

# Its Aftermath

When the plain-clothes men turned up, they checked all the names and addresses, took each person outside the door for questioning, and ascertained that, except for myself and the two unlucky hash-slingers, nobody had left the party until Bull brought Trickett out to speak to me. Then they let everybody else go, but hauled Trickett, myself, the caretaker and the two youngsters off to the nick to be questioned.

We were interviewed separately, of course, and they kept me until the last. I can't say that talking to a policeman who makes it obvious that he thinks you are lying is a pleasant experience. I heard later that they had soon let the youngsters go. All they wanted from them was the assertion that, so far as they knew, nobody except themselves, Bull and myself had been anywhere near the dark passage while the party was going on.

The interview with Trickett had taken longer. They had wanted full details about the Scottish tour, whether he had known Carbridge before he met him in Glasgow, why the students and Perth had left him and the others before the end of The Way and exactly where, when and why they had caught up with him again and, finally, where Perth was and why he had not accepted the invitation to the reunion.

On their part (said Trickett later) they had told him nothing, although he had asked point-blank how long Carbridge had been dead.

'That's for the inquest,' the detective-inspector told him. We all knew that, before the five of us had been ushered into the police cars, James Minch had been closely questioned, for he had given the rest of us a lively account of the interview before the five of us had been shipped off to the nick. It seemed, according to James Minch, that they suspected him of having had a *sgian dubh* tucked into his colourful woollen, right-leg stocking.

'You are also wearing a sporran, I see, sir.'

'It's an essential part of the outfit. No pockets in a kilt, you see.'

'I thought a dagger was also part of a Scotsman's native attire, sir.'

'A *dagger*? On the dance floor?'

'One of those small, ornamental knives they wear in their football-style socks, I meant.'

'Oh, a *sgian dubh*. I do have one at home, but I didn't bring it with me. As you see, I've nothing up the sleeve of my shirt, either, neither have I quarrelled with the deceased at any time or suffered any insults from him addressed either to my sister or myself.' (I was not too sure about this.)

'You don't speak with a Scottish accent, I notice.'

'It's been said, you know, that Scotsmen speak better English than the English.' (He himself spoke up-market Cockney.) 'In any case, I had the misfortune to be brought up in England and was educated at an English public school.'

'I think that is all I need trouble you with at present, then, though we may need to ask you some more questions about your knife at a later date, sir.'

'Why don't you ask Todd whether he's got a bomb tucked into the waistband of those elegant flannels? He's Bolshie-trained, you know — or is it IRA?'

'There is no need to be offensive, sir, either to me or Mr Todd.'

'But how to be offensive is the only thing I learned at my public school, Inspector. It *is* Inspector, isn't it?'

'Detective Chief Inspector Bingley, CID, to be exact, Mr Minch. You wear the kilt, but is Minch a Scottish name?'

'Probably of Norse origin, don't you think? North Minch, Little Minch — no, I couldn't say, but they're on the map. Our mother's name used to be Menzies, but nobody pronounces it correctly down here and we don't care for the Southern Cross rendering of it.'

'So your name is *really* Minch, but you are entitled to the tartan.'

'How horribly suspicious you make it sound! I almost wish our ancestors had not chosen it. Now that I come to consider the name closely, there is something pinchbeck about it. Oh, and my first name isn't James. It's Jamie. Just a fond father's foolishness, but one has no control over one's parents at the time of infant baptism. My sister's name is not Jane, but Jeanie, but she got tired of hearing my father singing "I dream of Jeanie with the light brown hair" — her own hair, as you may have noticed, being a rather resolute shade of red.'

'May I ask what your profession is, sir?'

'I collate, co-ordinate and, generally speaking, grapple with the organising of the collection of household waste in my borough, but I am hoping to stand for Parliament.'

Minch's eloquence and his ability to waste the inspector's time appeared not to have soured the man. Probably Minch had invented his share of the interview. Anyway, by the time he had finished with Trickett at the police station, the inspector was calm enough when it was my turn. However, urbane though he was with me, when at last my interview came, I did not like the experience one little bit. I had made up my mind not to tell him any more than he could gain by my answers to his questions and I hoped that neither Trickett nor Hera had told him anything about my discovery in the moorland ruins. It was soon apparent that, so far, they had not done so, but already I was regretting that I had babbled to Trickett. The fewer people who knew that, apparently, I was in the habit of discovering murdered corpses, the better it would be for me, I thought. All the same, the detective's first questions concerned the Scottish walk, although not, thank goodness, the row I had with Carbridge at Crianlarich.

'I understand that you met the rest of the party at the Glasgow youth hostel. Do you confirm that?'

'Yes, that's right.'

'Did you know any of the others beforehand?'

'My fiancée, Miss Camden, of course, and we had run into Todd at the airport hotel, but we didn't know him apart from that.'

'You and Miss Camden picked up the others again at Rowardennan, I understand.'

'Yes, that's right.'

'Why did you not travel more of the way with them?'

'An engaged couple need a bit of privacy. We had never had any intention of joining a party. The only reason we were ever with the rest of them was because we all used the same youth hostels, having no option.'

'Otherwise you and Miss Camden stayed in hotels.'

'And at Balmaha in separate cottages.'

'How did you get on with Mr Carbridge?'

'I didn't see enough of him to get on or not get on with him. I wrote him off as a rather irritating ass and a bit of a megalomaniac, that's all.'

'He seems to have had the reputation with his companions of being a good mixer.'

'Very likely. I wouldn't know.'

'Having been told on your invitation card or letter that this was to be a reunion party, were you surprised when Mr Carbridge did not turn up?'

'But he did turn up. He must have done, or I wouldn't have found him dead in that passage, would I?'

'Please confine yourself to answering my questions. What were you doing in that passage?'

'Falling over dead bodies, I suppose.' As soon as I had said it, I realised in what very bad taste it was. 'Sorry,' I said quickly. 'Actually, I had sneaked out to have a smoke.'

'A number of people seem to have been smoking in the dance-room, sir. Couldn't you have had your cigarette in there?'

'Yes, but it was noisy and overcrowded. I wanted some fresh air.'

'The passage you chose does not lead out to the fresh air.'

'The porter chap, Bull, thought I wanted the cloakroom.'

'Why should he have thought that, if you did not ask for it?'

'Because he's an officious idiot, I suppose.'

That, with my previous unfortunate remark, did it. I felt I had queered my pitch with the detective-inspector. However, we pressed on, or, rather, retraced our steps, since most of it was a repetition of what had gone before. I believe this is typical police procedure. They keep taking you over your story in the hope that you will change it in some way and give them a chance to pounce.

I realised that I had to be careful. I had to blot out from my mind the day we had lost our way in the mist. I summed him up as an experienced but not over-bright member of his profession. All the same, he was probably bright enough, owing to his experience, to know when a witness was holding out on him. I was made very much aware that this was the case when, having taken me through my story all over again, he said, 'Are you sure you have left nothing out, sir? What about the time between when you left Inveroran and arrived at the Kingsbridge hotel? That part of your trip seems to have taken a good deal of time.'

'For two reasons. First, we didn't set out very early – we had walked a long way since we left Drymen and, although we took The Way in easy stages day by day, I knew that Miss Camden was getting pretty tired. Secondly, we ran into a thick mist and were obliged to stay in a shepherd's hut until it cleared.'

'A shepherd's hut? You didn't mention that before, and you did not mention the mist.' As the hut was a complete fabrication, I knew I had to be extra careful at this point.

'We also spent a longer time than usual over lunch, but I can't see that any of this is important,' I said. 'The mist cleared and the rain came down, that's all. As for the time we took, well, what with the delay and the distance between Inveroran and Kingshouse and the fact that we had covered well over forty miles in just a few days and Miss Camden was tired – '

I realised that I was talking too much, so I stopped and then I said that that was how it had been.

'Just so,' he said, making a disquieting entry on the notes which he had in front of him on the table. 'Now, sir, holding the opinion of Mr Carbridge which you do — '

'*Did*,' I corrected him.

'Quite so. Holding this opinion which, as you stated it, is that he was' — he referred to his notes — "a rather irritating ass and a bit of a megalomaniac", why did you attend the reunion party at which, presumably, you expected to meet him again?'

This was an easy one and I answered it self-confidently.

'I wouldn't have accepted if the invitation had come from *him*, but it didn't. It came from the students and I would have hurt their feelings by refusing.'

'But did you expect to find Mr Carbridge at the gathering?'

'Oh, for heaven's sake, yes, but not by falling over his dead body!'

'Now, now, Mr Melrose, there is no need to be alarmed.'

But I felt that there was every need for this. He had realised that my last outburst was the result of fear and I could tell that he intended to exploit it. He did not do so at once. To my surprise, he thanked me for my help and dismissed me, merely adding that, if anything occurred to me which I thought he ought to know, he was sure that I would impart it to him.

I did not feel much like contacting Hera. Her last remarks had been anything but sympathetic. I did not blame her. Everybody had had a severe shock and hers must have been worse than anybody's except my own. I went straight back to my flat to brood over the situation and to wonder what other tricks Fate had tucked up its sleeve where I was concerned.

I had not been in for more than about half an hour before I had a caller. It was Trickett.

'There's going to be hell to pay over all this,' he said, when I had asked him in. I shared his gloom. 'How did you get on?' he asked, when I had poured out the drinks. 'What do you think that damn-fool policeman has done now? He's only rounded up the chaps and girls who played the pop music for us! As though they could have done that to Carbridge! So far as I know, they hadn't even met him.'

'I suppose the police have to question everybody who was on the premises,' I said. 'Not to worry about the orchestra people.

That detective may question them, but only as possible witnesses. The people he will put on the spot are the walking party and especially me. Look here, you won't let on that I found that other body, will you?'

'To be frank with you, Melrose, only if it comes to the crunch. I wish you hadn't told me about that, but the fact remains that you *did* tell me, so if one of our lot — the poly gang, you know — looks like taking the rap, well, you see what I mean.'

'Yes, I see what you mean and I can't say I blame you.' We both took a heartening gulp from our glasses. 'The trouble is,' I went on, 'that it must be somebody who was at the party. Nobody else would have known that Carbridge was going to be there.'

'I've been thinking about that. Carbridge must have had other acquaintances, you know, apart from those of us who were on the walk. Suppose he mentioned the party and the date and so on — these things pop up in casual conversation — and somebody who had a grudge saw a good chance to pay off old scores without being suspected?'

'How would the murderer have managed to get into your hall of residence?'

'By bluffing it out with Bull that he had been invited to the party, of course. Bull wouldn't have known any different. He knew me and Freddie and the two girls, Coral and Patsy, but nobody else except the members of the orchestra. They were all poly people, of course.'

'Another point: if Bull let the murderer and Carbridge in, they must have turned up early and anyway Bull must have seen the murderer. The police will have shown Bull the body — '

'They wouldn't need to. He and I both saw it before they came, if you remember. You went with us along that passage when I put in the new electric bulb. Bull saw the body then.'

'He didn't say he recognised it.'

'I bet he has said so by now.'

'And, of course, it's not very likely that Carbridge and his murderer turned up together. If you had planned to kill a chap, the last thing you would want would be to be seen in his company just before the deed was done.'

'The time factor bothers me a bit. The police aren't giving anything away, but it seemed likely that Carbridge was killed before the actual party got going. It looks as though he had an assignation with the murderer. I wish we knew how long he'd been dead when you fell over the body.'

'Why the hell it should have to be me, I can't think!' I exclaimed bitterly. 'I'd already fallen over one dead man. Why should it have to be two?'

'Well, they say coincidence has a long arm.'

'Not much comfort when the hand at the end of that arm has got you by the short hairs.'

'I think you might do worse than have a word with Bull. You can get him to tell you what he said to the police.'

'How is that going to help?'

'I don't know, but, in your shoes, I think I would want to know what people had been saying.'

'Well, what did *you* say?'

'Oh, that I had been responsible for organising the party and had written to everybody who was on the walk. I said that I had ended up at Fort William and that everybody who was there had climbed Ben Nevis except for you and Miss Camden. He rather pressed me as to why Perth had not come to the party and tried to tempt me into admitting that Perth and Carbridge had fallen out on The Way, but, of course, I wasn't having any of that, any more than I was telling him about Crianlarich. I knew about that punch-up, you know.'

'Do you mean they *had* fallen out — Perth and Carbridge?'

'In a manner of speaking, yes. That's one reason why our poly gang spent three days chipping away at the hills where you and Miss Camden found us. You see, we had already had a bit of a barney with him and Todd when we spent so much time on the island of Inchcailloch when *they* wanted to press on regardless and *we* wanted to study the geology of the island.'

'Couldn't they have gone on without you?'

'Both had taken a fancy to Patsy, I think. The girl wasn't

terribly interested, although perhaps a bit pleased just at first, the two men being a good deal older than Freddie and myself and, of course, employed, whereas we were only students. That meant they had a lot more money and, we gathered, assured positions with their firms.'

'You mean that Carbridge and Todd had fallen out?'

'Oh, I wouldn't go so far as that.'

'What, then?'

'Perhaps Patsy wasn't the only girl Carbridge had his eye on.'

I could not pretend that I did not know what he was hinting, but I said angrily, 'What the hell are you getting at?'

'Nothing, nothing — except that your Hera is a remarkably beautiful woman.'

'And engaged to be married to *me*, as I pointed out pretty forcibly to Carbridge at Crianlarich when he showed signs of muscling in. Yes, and to Todd, too.'

'Very sorry, Melrose. Didn't mean to rile you. More in the way of a warning, if you see what I mean.'

'Put your warnings where the monkey — '

'All right, all right.' He got up from his chair. 'Thanks for the drinks. See you at the inquest, I expect.'

When he had gone I went to the hall of residence. Bull let me in. I tackled him as soon as I got inside the door.

'Why didn't you tell me you recognised the dead man?' I asked.

'Recognise him? But I never, sir.'

'You let him in, and his murderer, too, on the afternoon of the party.'

'That I never did. If they got in, they got in *sub rosa*, sir. I hadn't never seen that corpse before in my life.'

'But how did he get in if you didn't let him in?'

'There's the basement entrance. That only gets locked and bolted at night.'

'Oh? Why is that?'

'I leaves it open during the daylight hours so I don't have to keep getting up on me pins to let in students as wants to work during the vaycaytions. Same in term-time. They comes and they goes. I got plenty of jobs to do without keep going along to answer the front-door bell. That's for visitors, not students. Them as come to the party was visitors, so, of course, I let 'em in if Mr Trickett was busy with the other guests, but I never let in that dead man. I've got a good memory for faces. Have to have, in my job. Why, I can remember students from ten years back, never mind about the lecturers.'

'The dead man had been invited to the party.'

'Well, he never come in by no front door, sir.'

When I got back to the flat, Bingley was waiting in the hall. We went up the stairs and I asked, rather belligerently, I think, whether there was any more that I could do for him.

'Just one small point, Mr Melrose,' he answered. 'What was your reaction when you first met Mr Carbridge at the Glasgow youth hostel?'

'I've told you. I thought him pushy and boring.'

'You would not care to add anything more?'

'There's nothing more to add. I thought the chap was a headache, that's all.'

'And you had no reason to revise this opinion later in the tour?'

'No. You must please believe what I've said before. Miss Camden and I did not travel in company with the others. It was only by chance that we met them in Glasgow and at the other youth hostels. They proposed to walk the whole length of the West Highland Way from Milngavie to Fort William. We had no such ambition. We picked up the trail at Drymen and, instead of keeping strictly to the route, we left out Kinlochleven and Lundavra, cut across to Ballachulish — having thumbed a lift — and were taken to Fort William from there. I've told you all this. Why do you keep harping on it?'

'Because, Mr Melrose, you did meet up with the others at Rowardennan, Crianlarich and Fort William.'

'Only because we all used the youth hostels, as I've already explained. There was no pre-arrangement to meet. Miss Camden and I were booked in mostly at hotels, but, of course, the hostels are much cheaper, so we used the only ones there are along The

Way, those at Rowardennan and Crianlarich and, of course, the one at Fort William, as you say.'

'I am told by Mr Todd that you and Miss Camden left Fort William in somewhat of a hurry. Was that because you found that Mr Carbridge was there?'

'Well, partly, I suppose, but mostly because Miss Camden had found our trip more exhausting than she had expected. We had intended to ascend Ben Nevis — I won't say *climb* it, because we only thought of getting to the top by the easiest route, which, as I am sure you know, is from the river up to a farm and then on a pony track to the top — but I decided that the exertion would be too much for Miss Camden. There was not much point in staying in Fort William under the circumstances, so we left as soon as we could.'

'Did you, at any time, have an altercation of any kind with Mr Carbridge?'

'Certainly not. I had nothing against him except that he was a bore.' (I certainly was not going to talk about Crianlarich to a policeman.)

'Was Miss Camden of the same opinion?'

'I should think everybody was, but you had better ask her, hadn't you? You're bad as young Trickett,' I said ill-advisedly. He stiffened, as I have seen a pointer do when it scents game.

'Ah,' he said, with a quiet satisfaction which alarmed me. 'Young Trickett, eh? Well, I think that is all for the present, Mr Melrose.'

I was more than thankful to be rid of him. I was terrified that I might let out our real reason for leaving Fort William. He had been so nearly right when he asked me whether we had left because Carbridge was there, and his penetrating question — although I do not think he had anything to go on when he asked it — of whether I had ever had any sort of a row with Carbridge had shaken me badly. I wondered what else Todd had told him, apart from recounting my hasty departure from Fort William. After all, Todd had been present when I had assaulted Carbridge at Crianlarich and had himself been fairly roundly ticked off by me as well. I did not imagine he loved me very much.

# 9

## Bull Before the Beaks

'How I detest that detective-inspector!' said Hera, when she and Sandy were having drinks at my flat and talking things over. 'Do you know he as good as told me that I had had an affair with Carbridge on the tour? How dare he?'

'He wanted me to admit that I knew about it and that I got shirty with the man,' I said. 'He's a menace with his rotten, crawling suggestions. He's got it in for me all right.'

'It's not as though you can help falling over dead bodies wherever you go,' she said thoughtfully.

'Look, the subject isn't funny!' I retorted.

'I didn't mean it to be but it *is* rather unnerving when you repeat your effects.'

'Mind you, if Bingley had known Carbridge, he would lay off this suggestion that you could have looked twice at the bloke,' I said. 'Now if it had been Todd — '

'What about Todd?' she asked sharply.

'Well, nothing except that he's a trier and people who try and try again do quite often succeed,' I said. I looked at her. She was thirty-one, but she appeared to be years younger. Her hair was as silken as that of a well-cared-for young child, her features were beautifully moulded, her hazel eyes were large and romantically soulful, but her mouth and chin were firm to the point of obstinacy. I have never seen a more self-contradictory face. That, and her perfect body, fascinated me.

'Well,' she said, 'are you having second thoughts about the goods in the shop window? Others may admire them more than you seem to do.'

'There have been times when I've liked you better,' I said,

but, when I had said this, her mood changed.

'We mustn't fight at a time like this,' she said. 'We're all being made to jump through hoops by that detestable detective-inspector. Take me out to dinner this evening and let's forget all about him and that boring man Carbridge, too, although I suppose I ought not to call him boring now that he's dead.'

'So far as I'm concerned,' I said, 'a dead Carbridge is about the least boring object I can think of at present. He's put us all in the cart.'

Sandy, who had been listening to the conversation without attempting to interrupt it, said that he was very glad not to have been at the party and that he did not like parties anyhow. Now that he had included himself in the discussion, he added that it was always useful to have somebody on the sideline who could follow the game without having to join in, and that what interested him most, apart from my involvement with the affair, was when and why the electric lightbulb in that passage had been removed.

'The murderer must have done that, and it was just your bad luck that you happened to be the first person to go along there,' he said kindly.

'And that only because the idiot of a caretaker or whatever he calls himself misdirected me,' I said. 'In any case he should have replaced that bulb. He knew that it had gone.'

'I suppose he didn't send you along the passage on purpose for you to find the body?' said Hera. 'I mean, when you come to think of it, he himself was by far the most likely person to have removed that electric lightbulb. He knew it had gone, as you say. If he's an innocent man, *why* hadn't he replaced it?'

'People do put off doing little jobs like that,' said Sandy. 'I expect he thought it would be time enough when term started.'

'But he knew there was a party in progress and people might need to go along that passage,' I pointed out.

'Well, I hope that beastly Bingley grilled him as well and truly as he did the rest of us,' said Hera.

'Nothing else will happen until after the inquest,' said Sandy. 'I suppose everybody was able to produce an alibi?'

'Alibis are useless when we don't know when the murder was committed,' I said, 'and Bingley has been as close as an oyster about that. Besides, you need witnesses to support an alibi.'

'Well, you and I are on safe ground there,' said Hera. 'Carbridge must have been killed before the party was properly in progress, perhaps immediately upon his arrival. Nobody supposes you went along that passage in the dark, murdered him without Bull hearing anything, and then went straight back and reported to him as caretaker that you had found a body. Anyway, you and I were in one another's company from about midday onwards. We shopped in Oxford Street, had lunch together, saw a film and then went on to the party. There must be plenty of people — shop girls, the waiter, the box-office girl, the cinema attendant, the taxi-driver who took us from the Haymarket to the poly hall of residence — who can swear to us.'

'That's true,' said Sandy, 'but you know what people are like. Ten to one, none of them will have taken enough notice to be able to remember you two.'

'You're not very complimentary to us,' said Hera. 'All the same, I don't trust Bingley an inch. He was perfectly beastly, in a smarmy kind of way, when he questioned me.' Her interview with him had been shorter than mine, but it appeared to have been conducted on much the same lines and she had had difficulty, she said, in concealing from him my discovery of the other body in the ruins, let alone the episode at Crianlarich.

'And I believe he knows I was fobbing him off,' she added. 'He may not be all that intelligent, but he's like a terrier at a rat-hole when it knows there's something there and is determined to get at it.'

'There's only one thing to do, if Comrie thinks he is likely to be in any kind of trouble,' said Sandy. 'You had better get Dame Beatrice on your side, Comrie.' I suppose we gazed at him, for he went on: 'Don't you see, man? This will be right up her street. You saw a body in Scotland and thought it was a dead Carbridge. You find another body in London and, dammit, it *is* a dead Carbridge. You'll be a classic case of ESP and meat and drink to a psychiatrist.'

'He says she has a wonderful cook and some vintage claret,' said Hera. 'He also speaks highly of a very attractive secretary. I'm not sure I want him to go there again.'

'The secretary is married and middle-aged,' I said. 'As for being a museum piece for a psychiatrist, that doesn't appeal to me either.'

'Well, there's an obverse and a reverse to every coin. If you really think that Bingley has cast you as the number one suspect — although you're probably quite wrong about that — why don't you appeal to Dame Beatrice's other great interest? She's a noted criminologist. She'll see you right if you are in trouble and are innocent.'

'Do you doubt my innocence?' I asked angrily. I was still raw from Bingley's questioning and some of Hera's criticism.

'Of course not, but I think you're mistaken about Bingley. He is bound to question everybody who was at the party. I wouldn't be a bit surprised to hear that he is chasing up that other fellow — you know, the students' bear-leader you told me about, the fellow who *didn't* go to the party. Now that's what I call a very suspicious circumstance. Why was he the only one not to turn up?'

'Considering that he lives in Scotland,' said Hera, 'I can quite understand that he wouldn't bother to come. I expect Bingley is quite satisfied with that explanation.'

'If anybody who *was* at the party killed Carbridge,' went on Sandy, 'surely it's far more likely to have been somebody who was with Carbridge all the time on that tour, rather than you, Comrie, or, come to that, you, Hera.'

'Hey!' said Hera.

'I was only using you as an instance. Now what about that chap Todd? From what you tell me, he and Carbridge teamed up right at the beginning of the tour — '

'And, according to what Trickett told me, fell out later when they both took a fancy to Patsy Carlow.'

'Patsy Carlow?' said Hera, laughing. 'What nonsense! Of course they didn't! How could they, when — '

'When *you* were there?' said Sandy. 'Yes, but, Hera dear, you

were there so little of the time, and, in any case, you were
bespoke. Both of them knew that.'

'Well, they didn't behave at Crianlarich as though they knew
it,' she said, looking at me.

'Oh, for heaven's sake!' I said. 'Can't we forget Crianlarich?'

'No more than Mary Tudor could forget Calais,' Hera answered.

'I think Hera has made her point,' said Sandy. 'Neither of the
men was really serious about Patsy.'

'Those Turkish trousers and the two-piece gilded bra!' said
Hera. 'Nobody could be serious about those or what was inside
them. Sorry! I'm being cheap and vulgar!'

'Yes, you are, rather,' I said, 'but, passing lightly on, suppose
we let Sandy pursue his theme. Men quarrel about things other
than girls.'

'I don't think I have any more to say, but I *do* think we
ought to keep Todd in mind. Didn't you say he was a former
member of the poly hall of residence? That means he was no
stranger to that passage.'

'He's also tall enough to have removed that lightbulb without
using a ladder,' I said. 'He could have known that the students'
entrance was always kept unlocked until dark, so it was available to anybody who knew the ropes. What is more, there is a
back staircase up from the students' entrance to the passage
where I found Carbridge's body.'

'So Todd could have taken Carbridge into the house that
way, led him into the passage and murdered him — ' said
Sandy.

'And then removed the lightbulb, leaving the body in a dark
passage all ready for Comrie to fall over it,' said Hera.

'It sounds the perfect solution. Oh, Sandy, do go on!'

'I think not,' said Sandy. 'Let's get the inquest over and then
I'll make my point. Once we are told exactly when Carbridge
died, we shall know where everybody stands.'

The inquest did not take long. As no relatives of the dead
man had shown up, the body was formally identified by Todd
and nothing else was taken except the medical evidence. Here
the police surgeon was backed up by the pathologist who had

made a more detailed examination of the body. Their conclusions did not help very much. Death could have occurred
four hours or even more before the police surgeon saw the body
and the time factor was complicated by the fact that — as we
discovered for the first time — the murderer had attempted to
strangulate Carbridge before finishing him off with a fatal stabbing. All the same, it still looked as though the attack must have
been made before the party had begun and I said as much to
Sandy. He agreed.

'Yes,' he said, 'Carbridge must have got there early and, if he
did, so did somebody else, of course. The question is — why?'

'I don't suppose we shall ever know why.'

The verdict at the inquest was murder by person or persons
unknown. Three days later I read in the paper that Bingley had
arrested Bull, the caretaker.

'Bingley must be crazy,' I said, 'or else his superiors have
been leaning on him and he felt he had to make a quick arrest.
It's true that a foolish chap such as Carbridge seems an unlikely victim, but murdered he was, so somebody must have
done it. All the same, Bull seems even more unlikely as a murderer. I could understand Bingley's action if Bull had mistaken
Carbridge for an unlawful intruder and coshed him. I expect
these caretaker chaps keep a bludgeon of some sort handy in
these lawless times. Cold steel between the shoulders doesn't
fit the picture, somehow, and as for a chap of Bull's age trying
(and pretty near succeeding) to throttle a younger man — '

'The police must have something to go on. They don't arrest
people on no grounds whatever. What was Bull doing, did you
say, when you first spoke to him?' asked Sandy.

'Sitting at a little table eating fish and chips and reading a
newspaper.'

'I should think the magistrates would dismiss the charge
when he's brought before them.'

'I doubt that very much. Murder is such a dreadful matter
that they will be bound to treat it seriously. Besides, the defence
will reserve their evidence and when that happens the thing is
sure to go to trial. I feel as though I'm partly responsible for the

poor fellow's arrest. I wish anybody but I had found the body.'

'Yes, that was your bad luck, as we've said before, but it doesn't matter who found it. Bull would still have been arrested. Surely nobody else would have been on the premises four hours, or more, before the party was due to kick off.'

'Oh, wouldn't they, though!' I said. 'We have been told that students had access all day if they wanted to get on with some work.'

'It was a Saturday, remember.'

'Even so, I doubt whether that would count for anything if a student had a job to finish — mounting and labelling specimens or photographs, something pleasant and interesting of that sort, perhaps. Don't forget, either, that lots of shops close at one o'clock on Saturdays, so there could have been students coming in with provisions and drinks for the party. I don't think Bull was the only pebble on the beach that Saturday afternoon.'

'But if there was all that coming and going, how would the murderer not have been spotted?'

'Because — I've been thinking about that while we've been talking — because of where the throttling was actually carried out. Remember where the dark passage led? I think the first attack was made in the Gents. Then the murderer removed the body to the passage with the intention of leaving it there for somebody else to find when he had removed the electric light-bulb. He must have had a bit of a facer when he discovered that Carbridge was not quite dead. He knew that he dared not let him recover, hence the stabbing.'

'With a knife already in his possession?'

'Lots of fellows carry knives quite legitimately. We don't know what kind of knife the murder weapon was. I suppose the police have kept that a secret until it's produced at the trial.'

'I didn't see a knife sticking out of the body, but I didn't look very closely. His face was enough for me. Strangulation isn't a very lovely thing to gaze upon.'

'I sympathise with you. Horrible!'

'Yes, it certainly was. I wonder what the police had to say to those two students?'

'What two students?'

'The boy and girl who were slinging the food-stuffs about. They must have gone past the entrance to the passage half a dozen times or more while the party was in progress and past Bull's table in that corridor. According to the medical evidence, the weapon found sticking in the body was a very ordinary kitchen knife, but they don't specify what kind of kitchen knife. I mean, they come in all sizes and have various uses. From the interest the police took in James Minch and his *sgian dubh*, I visualise a small vegetable knife. There must be one in every kitchen in the land and it would be very difficult to trace this one to its natural home, for I bet it didn't come from the hall of residence kitchen.'

'And even if it had,' said Sandy, 'the two students who were operating in that kitchen on the day of the party wouldn't have missed it. There were no vegetables to prepare.'

'Of course there were! What about peeling and chopping up the onions for the hamburgers?'

'Do you put onions with ham?'

'The original hamburgers were named after Hamburg, I believe, and did not contain ham. They incorporated minced steak and chopped onions. I remember eating one at, of all places, the London Zoo when England first took to them.'

The set-up at the police court was in some respects like that at the inquest and in some ways very different. For one thing there seemed to be police everywhere. This, and the number of solicitors present, could be accounted for by the fact that Bull's case was only one of several which were to be heard that morning, although none of the others dealt with an accusation of murder.

In place of the coroner, his clerk and the medical witnesses, there was a bench of five magistrates, and in front of them at a lower level sat the magistrates' clerk and a couple of typists. The press was well represented, too, and the public gallery was full. Escorted by a policeman who remained with him during the proceedings, Bull appeared in the dock from down below, where I suppose the cells were, and in place of the coroner's jury there were Bingley and his sergeant, and next to where they sat was the witness box.

A selection of drunks, muggers and petty pilferers, together with a couple of motorists who had exceeded the speed limit in a built-up area, were all dealt with before it came to Bull's turn. He had been produced in answer to a succession of what appeared to me to be totally unnecessary police calls, and the policeman acting as warrant officer gave the magistrates the case number.

Bull was asked whether his name was Henry Thomas Bull, agreed that it was and then Bingley read out the charge. Bull pleaded Not Guilty and then the prosecuting solicitor told the story and I was called from the public gallery to bear witness to the discovery of Carbridge's body. I took the oath, agreed to my name and to the date on which the party had been held.

'What were you doing when you discovered the body?'

'I was going along to have a cigarette.'

'Were you acquainted with the layout of the premises?'

'No, I had never been there before.'

'What made you go down an unlighted passage?'

'Just chance, I suppose. I was looking for a way out to the open air.'

'And in the passage you stumbled over the body?'

'Yes.'

'What did you do then?'

'I struck a match and saw that it was Carbridge.'

'I will take you back to the previous answer. You say you were not familiar with the premises?'

'That's right.'

'Yet you chose to go blundering down a totally unlighted passage?'

'Yes.'

'Why? You might have encountered any number of obstacles. You could see nothing in the darkness, could you?'

'No, or I should not have stumbled over the body.'

'Quite so. So why did you choose to go down the passage?'

I had done what I could to keep Bull's name out of my answers, but it was clear that the solicitor knew the truth and was determined to get it out of me. I capitulated, for my own sake. I did not see the fun of being charged as Bull's accessory through being obstructive.

'As a matter of fact,' I said, 'I was following directions given me.'

'By whom?'

'By Bull. I ought to say that he gave them with the kindest intentions. He thought I wanted to be directed to the men's cloakroom, which I now know is at the end of the passage.'

That was about the lot, so far as I was concerned. There were questions about how long and how well I had known Carbridge and also about the drinks we had had at the party, but over all this I had nothing to hide. The next witness was the policeman who had first been called to look at the body. According to custom, he was not questioned, but, having taken the oath, he gave a straightforward factual account of his actions, and the defending solicitor was asked whether he had any questions to put to the officer.

There were none, and the medical evidence came next. Here there was a surprise in store for all of us. Having agreed that the deceased had died of a stab wound delivered from the back, the pathologist went on to provide forensic chapter and verse. There was no doubt that Carbridge had been stabbed in the heart, after there had been a very determined attempt to strangle him. When the defending solicitor took over, his first question was: 'Did anything about the nature of the wound surprise you?'

'Nothing about the nature of the wound itself, but I was surprised, when I made a more detailed study of the body after it had been removed by ambulance, to discover that the weapon actually found in the wound was not, in my opinion, the weapon which had been employed to complete the murder.'

From my seat on the public benches I saw Detective-Inspector Bingley suddenly stiffen and half rise. The chairman of the bench noticed this, too, and so did the solicitor. Everybody could understand the importance of this statement: if a second weapon had been inserted in place of the murder weapon, the death need not have occurred either in the passage or, indeed, even at the hall of residence, although that it had taken place elsewhere seemed unlikely. The danger of transporting a dead man through the streets of London by daylight was incalculable and would only have been attempted by a madman.

The defending solicitor then asked the pathologist whether, for the benefit of their worships, he could produce any evidence to support his statement.

'Yes,' he replied. 'I called in my colleague, Professor Antonio Corelli, the eminent pathologist who is now attached to St Hubert's Hospital.'

'Is the professor in court?'

'Yes, he is.' So Professor Antonio Corelli was called and, in such precise English that anybody would have known that he was a foreigner, backed up the statement that the murder weapon was not the weapon which had been left sticking in between the shoulders of the corpse.

'Can you suggest what the nature of the murder weapon was?'

'Except that it had a broader blade than the weapon which the murderer had then driven into the wound, no, I cannot. I could hazard a guess, but it might be misleading, so I shall say nothing of such speculations. What I *will* say is — ' He went on to give all the pathological details. As he produced chapter and verse, less and less could I see Bull going for trial. The weapon in the wound had been a small kitchen knife and marks on the end of the handle indicated that the point of the knife had been inserted in the slightly torn edges of the original aperture and then the end of the handle had been struck a shrewd blow with a hammer or other implement to drive it well into the wound. The pathologist could even add a little more. The original weapon had been double-edged. The kitchen knife was sharp only along one edge. The cook at the hall of residence was called. She testified that her tally of kitchen cutlery was complete. She added that Bull lived on the premises and had access to the kitchen, 'as he takes his elevenses and his meals with us, nor a milder-mannered man, no matter what his previous occupation might have been, and him proud of it and anyway somebody got to do them things and a big mistake ever to have done away — '

'Yes, yes, thank you, Mrs Geard. You may step down now.' She was followed by the two students, Freddie and Coral, who had used the kitchen to prepare the food for the party, but they had nothing useful to tell the court. They had been in and out of the kitchen a good many times, had passed the entrance to the passage but had not been along it and had no idea that the electric lightbulb had disappeared.

The magistrates retired. When they came back, the chairman said, 'In view of what we have heard, and taking all the circumstances into account, we find that there is insufficient evidence on which to commit this man for trial.'

'Well!' said Bull explosively. 'I could have told you that without all this gas and gaiters and holding of me in custody like a common criminal. I been a man of the law meself in my time, I'd have you to know, and — '

'Be quiet, man!' said the chairman of the bench, 'and think yourself lucky. I am warning you that this is a reprieve, not an acquittal. There is nothing to prevent your being rearrested at a later date, if the police produce fresh evidence against you.'

# 10

## The Disperser of Dreams

Once the magistrates had refused, on the evidence (if one can call it that) given at the hearing, to commit Bull for trial, the heat, of course, was on the rest of us again.

So far as Bingley was concerned, I think that, for a time at least, Bull remained the chief suspect, but I am sure I came next on the list. It still seems to me illogical that this should be so. All I had done, so far as he was aware, was that I had found the body and reported the fact. It was not as though he knew anything about what had happened at Crianlarich or the strange business of the body in the ruins on Rannoch Moor.

Todd was also being pestered. Hera rang me up when I got back from the office one evening to tell me that Todd had turned up at her flat and wanted to have a talk with me.

'Then why didn't he come here instead of going to your place?' I asked.

'He didn't know when you got home from work.'

'A likely excuse! All right, I'll come round, but I can't stay long. I've brought a manuscript home with me and Sandy wants my opinion on it as soon as I've read it. Be seeing you in about a quarter of an hour and you take jolly good care that Todd leaves when I do. I don't trust that picker-up of unconsidered trifles.'

'So *that's* what you think I am!'

'Forget it.'

Todd was tall, debonair and handsome — all the things, in fact, that I am not. He was also beautifully attired and his manners were impeccable.

'How are you?' he said. 'Bearing up all right?'

'I might be, if that perishing policeman would get off my neck.'

'Ah, you, too,' he said, standing up as Hera came into the room with the drinks. He took the tray from her, set it down and added, 'Poor old Bull is being needled, too. Too bad, after the beaks dismissed him without a stain on his character.'

'I wouldn't put it quite like that,' I said. 'He was guilty of dereliction of duty. He ought to have replaced that bulb as soon as he knew it had gone. When did he know it had gone, I wonder?'

'I've been talking to him. The policeman has rather dwelt on the point, of course, and Bull told me what he told him and he swears it's the truth. He did not discover it had gone until about two in the afternoon, when he needed to visit the what-have-you. He pressed the switch and no light came on, so he uttered a bold word, cursing whatever student had pinched the bulb for one of the study-bedrooms, and went up the stairs to a loo on the second floor. After that, he says, he was kept on the trot by the people who were giving the party and, although he fully intended to replace the bulb, it meant fetching a ladder (as he is too short to manage without one) and for a time he was kept so busy running back and forth for the party preparations that — well, one can see how it would have been.'

'But when I went along that corridor to have a fag, the blighter was doing damn-all except reading a newspaper and eating fish and chips. Resting after his labours, I suppose. Anyway, what has Bingley got on you that you wanted to talk to us about?'

'That silly little clot Patsy Carlow has given the coppers reason to believe that Carbridge and I were rivals in love — love for *her*, if you please!'

'Well, those Turkish pantaloons were really rather eye-catching. Had either of you seen her in them before?' asked Hera. 'I thought they were very fetching.'

'Ripeness is all,' said Todd, 'if you're going to flaunt yourself in that sort of garb, and pathetic young Patsy is hardly Mata Hari. However, to your question, so far as I am concerned the answer is no. Unfortunately, of course, the middle-aged Bingley saw her in those Turkish reach-me-downs when he came in and broke up the party that Saturday, and apparently was struck all of a heap. The result is that he believes her story that Carbridge and I were wildly infatuated with her and that we fell out because of this. I told him that at the party my reaction to the bizarre garments was to give her a fatherly smack on the seat of them, and what do you suppose he said when I told him that?'

'I can't wait to know,' said Hera.

'He said, "Sexy, Mr Todd, very sexy." '

'Well, apparently there are the three of us on his roster,' I said. 'What do you expect me to do about it? I can't extricate myself, let alone anybody else.'

'I know. Safety in numbers, though. As long as he's got three of us under suspicion — well, it's better than only one. What I wanted to say was that I've told him nothing about that little affray at Crianlarich and I shan't, either, unless I have to. You know what I mean.'

'Perfectly. Neither will I mention Jane Minch's sore feet,' I said, risking a shot in the dark. It went home, though.

He looked at me in a speculative way and said, 'So you worked that one out, did you?' He finished his drink and got up to go. 'So it's checkmate, is it?'

'Let us say, with Mr Peachum, "you know we have it in our power to hang each other". Anyway, thank goodness the law doesn't go quite so far as that nowadays.'

'Amen,' he said, 'but I think it's only a matter of time, you know.'

'So what on earth were you getting at?' asked Hera, when she had shown him out. 'How did you get him sewn up like that?'

'Easily. It stands to reason that, once Jane's feet began to trouble her, the rather insensitive and egotistic Carbridge would have insisted upon pushing ahead and leaving the brother and sister behind.'

'They were all at Fort William.'

'So were Perth and the students. My guess is that everybody except Carbridge and Todd got a lift or took the bus for the end part of the trip. That means those two blokes were alone to-gether for the last part of The Way. From friend Todd's reac-tions, I should say that my faculty of imagination, plus a logical and analytical mind, has paid dividends.'

'You are cleverer than I thought. It must come from reading so many books,' she said mockingly. 'What else have you deduced?'

'That Todd is a snake in the grass.' She turned colour, so I added, 'I quite like him, though, and I have nothing against snakes. Their venom has curative properties when it's put to therapeutic use.'

It was after this that I began to have bad dreams. I suppose most people have them at times, but to me they came as an unwelcome novelty. Mostly my dreams, when I could remember them in the morning, were of the most trivial content — I had dressed wrongly for some function or had found myself on a lonely road with no idea of how I had come to be there or in which direction I ought to be going. The worst dream I had had up to the night which followed the hearing at the police court and the talk with Todd, was that my and Sandy's authors had turned into a pack of wolves and invaded the office thirsting for my blood.

The new dreams were very much worse than that. For one thing, they persisted night after night and they were horrifying. I dreamt that Todd — strangely enough not Carbridge — had turned into the Ancient Mariner's albatross and was hanging from my neck. I could not rid myself of him and he was stifling me with his weight.

After the fourth night of this, Hera asked me what was wrong. She thought I must be sickening for something and advised me to see a doctor. Sandy was more sympathetic and to him I told my troubles.

'It isn't a doctor I need,' I said. 'It's something in the nature of an exorcist.'

'Well, you're on the books of one,' he said. 'Go and see her. Of course it's not Todd you're dreaming about.'

'You mean I've substituted him for Carbridge, but I don't

think that is the case. After all, I'm not really concerned in the murder, you know — not personally, I mean. I'm sorry for any man who dies before his time, but I'm not involved beyond that.'

'You've had a couple of very nasty shocks, whether your conscious mind recognises that fact or not. Then you had the harassment of believing that Bingley suspected you. You go along to Dame Beatrice — '

'And have my head looked at?'

'Yes, if you care to put it like that.'

Hera offered to accompany me, but I thought I should do better on my own. I said I was not going to keep her away from her job. She had some lucrative modelling on hand and I knew she did not want to lose the chance of it. Fortunately she was only too willing to listen to reason, so, having made an appointment, I went alone, as before, to the Stone House.

'Ah,' said Dame Beatrice, when I had described my recurrent dream, 'and how old were we when we first encountered the Ancient Mariner and his albatross?'

Her reptilian smile and her use of the royal, the editorial and the specialist's plural, impressed me about equally and not very deeply. I knew it was a joke.

'I was ten and at my prep school,' I said. 'I had a woman teacher and she did not beat us for our misdemeanours, but caused us to learn poetry by heart. If we failed to come up to scratch, we were sent to the headmaster as stubborn recusants and he *did* beat us, so, of course, we learnt the stuff, however hard a grind it turned out to be.'

'I see. Have you discussed this dream with your fiancée?'

'No. I've told my business partner about it.'

'So he is your good friend as well as your business partner. What had he to say?'

'Well, rather strangely he said that the dream was not really about Todd. He said I was substituting Todd for someone else.'

'I am sure he was right. In fact, I think you are substituting Todd for two other people. If you will not take my supposition amiss, I think one of them is your fiancée.'

'Hera? Oh, no, I assure you!'

'I am glad to hear that.' She did not look very glad. In fact, those brilliant black eyes summed me up very shrewdly indeed and it was not difficult to imagine what she was thinking. She was right, too, although I was not prepared to admit it. I *did* find being engaged to Hera something of an onus at times. Her character was so much firmer than my own that I was often at a disadvantage when we discussed anything or argued about it. But Dame Beatrice had more to say. 'What ought you to have told me about Mr Carbridge when last you were here?'

So I told her what had happened at Crianlarich. She nodded solemnly and then suddenly cackled.

'You would have preferred to punch Mr Todd, I suppose, but, to employ a phrase much used by Laura, he is above your weight, a taller and a more robust man than yourself.'

'I wasn't going to let Hera see me take a hiding.'

'Very wise. A jousting knight must win or retire from the lists.'

'Besides, although I somewhat distrust Todd, he doesn't irritate me in the way Carbridge did.'

'Well, Mr Melrose, we will take it that you are suffering from suppressed hysteria due to your recent disquieting experiences. With your collaboration, I shall place you under light hypnosis and then I shall talk to you. You may answer me if you wish, but you will remember nothing of what we say, and the dream you have described will not recur. However, as I read the evidence, I do not think that at present you are very anxious to be married.'

'Well, I am and I'm not,' I said truthfully.

'Elucidate.'

'Well, I'm very fond of Hera and I admire her very much, but when we announced our engagement to my business partner, Hera added that she wanted to come into the firm. She has some capital and I was willing to consider the idea, although I was not too keen on it, but Sandy was not at all in agreement, so that damped me down a bit. The last thing I want is any kind of a break with him.'

'Your business needs an infusion of money?'

'Well, I suppose most businesses do, but I don't much want Hera to go out to work after we're married. I pointed out to her that it would be jollier to find her all nice and domesticated at home when I got back each evening.'

'A typical male reaction, of course, selfish, possessive, hidebound and utterly understandable. I wonder whether she expected to be a sleeping partner or an active partner in your business?'

'Well, that's where Sandy and I are not in agreement. I say she would only be a sleeping partner drawing her small share of the profits and staying out of the office. I say that she will take no part in making decisions or even meeting any of our authors. They show up from time to time and take us out to lunch or we take them out to lunch — that kind of thing. Sometimes they come to raise hell about their contracts and try to sick us on to get to grips with their publishers, but it's all in the day's work and I don't intend Hera to be a part of it.'

'How does your partner see her role, then?'

'Sandy says women are never satisfied unless they've got a finger in the pie. I'm bound to admit that in Hera's case he may be right.'

'Difficult for you. Shall we proceed?'

So I suffered her to put me under what she called 'light hypnosis' and all that I remembered afterwards was the sound of her beautiful voice reciting poems from *Peacock Pie* before I came under the influence. What magic formula she used, once she had me under control, I have no idea. When I came to, we had tea, at which we were joined by Laura, and I drove back to London feeling calm and refreshed. I slept that night, and for many nights, without, so far as I can remember, dreaming at all. It was only after waking in the mornings that I wondered what I had told Dame Beatrice.

'So you didn't talk about the bodies,' said Sandy.

'I have no recollection of what we talked about. If the body on Rannoch Moor had been a figment of my imagination, I might still be worried, but what I found was a real man. I mistook him for Carbridge, that's all. I had given my head quite a bash, you know. There was only one thing about the interview which worried me a little. Well, not worried me exactly, but made me feel a bit of a fool.'

'Dame Beatrice's diagnosis about hysteria, I suppose.'

'Yes. Previously I had connected hysteria only with nervous females.'

'What about shell-shock? If she had used that word to describe your condition, you wouldn't have minded. Now I'll tell you something else. You've been under stress for some time. I noticed it before you ever went on that Scottish jaunt, and now these two encounters of yours with murdered men have triggered off something which has been dormant for months. Why didn't you tell Dame Beatrice what is really worrying you? — or you could tell *me*. We're both safe enough as the repositories of guilty secrets.'

'But I haven't got any guilty secrets, dammit! All the same, I'm not too sure now that I ought to have agreed to hypnosis. I mean, it makes one so vulnerable.'

'Think nothing of it. She would never make any capital of anything she learned that way; no doctor would. The point is — has her treatment worked?'

'Like a charm, so far.'

'Well, then, what are you worried about?'

'I'll tell you. Now that Bull has been cleared — '

'Oh, but he hasn't, you know. I thought the head beak made that abundantly clear. Bull has been put back into circulation, but only while Bingley gets more evidence. If what you tell me about Bingley is a correct assessment, he's not the man to let go while he's got his teeth into a suspect. You know that, as well as I do. You've said as much.'

'There's something Bingley doesn't know, unless somebody has tipped him off. I've been waiting and dreading the day when it comes out that I had a row with Carbridge at Crianlarich.'

'Well, you told me you had one with Todd, and he's still alive.'

'Yes.'

'Could anybody else in the party have known about the quarrels?'

'Not unless Carbridge himself had talked. Unfortunately, he was the sort of gregarious babbler who very easily might have done. Oh, I suppose Perth knew — and possibly the Minches.'

'If anybody knew and had blabbed to Bingley, you would have heard about it long before this, but no wonder you've been worried. No wonder, either, that it was Carbridge you thought you had found on Rannoch Moor. I understand everything now. Let's talk about something else. I've got my problems too, you know. This business of you and Hera. She's been on to me again about joining the firm and having a partnership. I still don't like the idea, Comrie. I don't want any takeover bids and Hera is a very determined woman.'

'She won't kick in enough capital to make her anything but a very junior partner. We could do with a bit more money, couldn't we?'

'Well, yes, but in this case I'm sure the interest we should have to pay in the form of her making a takeover bid would be too high. Would you mind very much if I turned her offer down very determinedly indeed? We've stalled, up to the present, but I'm willing to bear the brunt of telling her firmly that there's nothing doing. I quite see that it would be very embarrassing for you if you had to slip her the news.'

'We'll stick together over this. I am altogether of your point of view, although I shall have to involve you to some extent, of course.'

'Help yourself. It won't break *this* camel's back if you load me up.'

'After all, I don't want her running round in this office, and that for more reasons than one. For one thing, as I've told her, I want her home when I get there after a hard day's work. I've always said so to her.'

I envisaged a stormy interview but, although she set her lips and tilted that obstinate chin, she took my arguments calmly.

'You may think differently when we are married, if ever we are,' she said. 'I believe you've cooled off.'

'I'm only waiting for you to fix the date,' I told her.

'I've got commitments for the autumn, but some time in the New Year ought to be all right. And don't worry about me and your agency. I knew, before we went to Scotland, that Sandy would talk you over.'

'Nothing of the sort! You know very well that I want a wife, not a business partner. That's the size of it.'

'I could be both, but never mind.'

I gave Sandy the news that I was to be married in the New Year and that I had been firm about the partnership.

'How did she take it?' he asked.

'Fairly lamb-like. She's disappointed, of course, but she has accepted the situation with more grace than I thought she would. She said she knew what our decision would be.'

'Since when?'

'Since before she and I went on that tour — or so she said. She must have had the partnership in mind for months.'

'Oh, well, now she will have a good many weeks to get used to the idea that she is not joining the firm. Nothing like a bit of a cooling-off time to resolve these little difficulties. Women are far more reasonable and amenable than men over business arrangements. By the time you're married, everything will be all right.'

I was not too sure that either 'reasonable' or 'amenable' applied to Hera, but I did not argue. She had agreed with our decision, that was all that mattered — and she had given me a tentative date for our wedding. I noticed that she and Sandy had both mentioned 'cooling off', but I dismissed the doubts I had begun to feel when I visited the Stone House and which, I admit, I had experienced while I was in Scotland; and I felt grateful to Hera for having so far accepted our refusal to take her into partnership. I even began to read the advertisements of houses for sale in the more desirable commuter districts. I had no intention that Hera and my children should live in London and, in any case, I did not want her too near the office. She had formed a habit of 'dropping in' when she was not otherwise engaged, and this I intended to do my best to check when we were married.

However, even this inconvenient habit she ceased entirely after our talk. We met for dinner most evenings, sometimes at my flat — where my housekeeper was quite pleased to cater for two instead of one, especially as we had an arrangement that I should pay her a little extra on these occasions, and that she should get off early and leave the washing-up until the morning. Sometimes I dined with Hera, who did her own delicious cooking when she was at home. Mostly, however, we went out for the meal and then spent the rest of the evening, and occasionally the night, together, either at her place or mine. All my qualms about marrying her vanished and about three happy weeks went by with no unpleasant surprises and no evil dreams. Bingley, of course, was still about, but even he and his suspicions troubled me no longer.

## 11

## *Mugdock Wood or Thereabouts*

This interval of comparative peace gave me a chance of settling down to work again. I enjoyed my job and had always got on well not only with Sandy but with our office staff, so that everything connected with the agency always went smoothly except for an occasional breeze created by a dissatisfied author. These rufflings of the waters we had learned to encounter without trepidation, for they soon blew over and normal conditions were restored.

We had not, so far, worked the agency up to the stage where we could decline to represent an author until he had had at least one publication to his credit, but we had several good old faithfuls whose work we could always sell and Sandy had begun to talk hopefully of going over to America to canvass the possibilities of starting a branch of our business in the States.

What sometimes caused me a little disquiet was Hera's changed behaviour and attitude towards me. I was not surprised any longer by her calm acceptance of our veto on a partnership for her. I guessed that she was biding her time until a new opportunity presented itself for a further onslaught on our defences. Sandy thought the same.

'She has taken it much too well,' he said, 'for a woman who does not like to be thwarted. I hope she is all right – not sickening for anything or considering going into a nunnery or becoming a missionary or anything of that sort?'

'If so, she doesn't mention it. As for her health, she could not possibly be more blooming. She is lively and entertaining, has an excellent appetite and says she sleeps well.'

'Says?'

'She thinks we ought to pack that sort of thing up now until we are married. I'm in full agreement, so I have only her word for how well she sleeps.'

'It didn't seem to suit you too well on your Scottish tour.'

'It was different then. We were together all day and every day, so it seemed strange to part at night. Under present circumstances, I'm all in favour of holding off until after the wedding.'

He eyed me and said, 'Hm! Fancy that, now!'

'Meaning what?'

'Just hoping that abstinence, like absence, makes the heart grow fonder.'

'She is much more companionable, less censorious and certainly more beautiful than I've ever known her.'

'Bless you, my innocent boy!'

'Meaning what?' I asked for the second time.

'Devious creatures, the females of the species. Speaking probably out of turn, but as an old friend and well-wisher, don't you wonder what she's up to?'

'I know what she's up to, and you and I have both given voice to it. It's the lull before the storm. She hasn't given up hope of storming this little fortress of ours. You don't need to warn me about that. I'm quite ready for the bombardment when it comes. No, what worries me is the bloom on her cheeks and the light in her eyes.'

'That's what I meant,' he said. 'Watch out and don't forget my holiday is due very soon. I shan't be on hand to espouse your cause once I go on furlough.'

It was my turn to hold the fort while Sandy went on holiday. Even before I met Hera, one of the disadvantages of the agency had been that he and I could never take our holidays together as we had always done in the halcyon days at college. A week before he was due to take his three weeks' leave I enquired what his plans were, for it was unlike him not to have mentioned them earlier. Usually he was full of enthusiasm and Hera and I knew weeks beforehand where he had decided to go and what he proposed to do when he got there.

'My holiday?' he said, when I mentioned it. 'Oh, I'm going to walk the West Highland Way. You might lend me that rucksack of yours. No point in my buying one, is there?'

So I lent him the rucksack, my ashplant, my electric torch, my whistle and my maps and saw him off at Euston. I would have lent him my anorak and my nailed boots had they fitted him, but he is a big fellow with very wide shoulders and large feet. I was astonished when he told me that he was planning to walk The Way. His taste was for the exotic and he was, so far as he could afford to be, a sybarite, revelling in first-class cabins on cruises, luxury hotels on the French Riviera and beaches in the Bahamas. He lived quietly, almost frugally, all the year and then broke into a cascade of fireworks on holiday.

I suppose I looked as astonished as I felt, for he said defensively that I had made The Way sound very attractive, that he had some extra poundage of which he was determined to rid himself and that a man needed to commune with Nature from time to time if he wanted to retain possession of his immortal soul.

'So what's the real reason?' I asked. He laughed.

'You disbelieving old so-and-so!' he said; but he offered no answer to the question.

When I told Hera, she said, 'We've whetted his curiosity, that's all. What a pity I've got to be in Paris next week. I could have come and helped you in the office. If it weren't for Sandy, you would take me into partnership, wouldn't you?'

It was the first I had heard of the Paris trip, but I blessed it. I had no mind to allow her to get her foot in at the office, so I did not answer her question. I was uneasy, however, for her remark indicated that she had not given up hope of being taken into partnership and I still envisaged stormy seas ahead.

'Oh, Sandy only expects to take a week, or very little longer, on the walk,' I said. 'Then he'll pop back here for a couple of days to pack for Stockholm.'

'What on earth does he want with Stockholm? I thought he never went on holiday further north than Funchal or Cannes.'

'There's a book fair. Some of our authors are represented, so he thinks one of us ought to show up. When do you set off for Paris?'

'Tomorrow. You and Sandy will be busy if he's going on Wednesday, so don't come and see me off. There will be a party of us, all women except for Maurice, and you can't stand *him*.'

Sandy had never written to me when he was on holiday, so I was very much surprised to get a letter in a large envelope with his unmistakable superscription on it, particularly as I should be seeing him again so soon. He had arranged to drop in at the office the day after he got back from Scotland and pick up some papers to take with him to Stockholm. He had gone off on the Wednesday and the letter came on the following Wednesday morning. It contained some very startling news which I might have found incredible except for my own experiences north of the Border and subsequently in London. He wrote:

'This is in the form of a diary, as I want a record of my experiences. You might lock it away somewhere when you've read it. I shall have been discharged from hospital and on my way home. Not to worry and don't tell Hera. No harm done and no bones broken and shall be joining you soon after you get this.

'*Wednesday*. An easy train journey north by way of Warrington, Wigan, Preston, Lancashire and Carlisle. Put up at Renfrew for the night. Good room and good dinner. Hotel full, but much coming and going, as everybody very much a bird of passage. Met up with Mellish after dinner and we had a drink together. He goes on to Perth tomorrow. You remember him from college, I expect.

'*Thursday*. Took a bus to Milngavie to start the walk. As I went to get on board in Buchanan Street, some careless oaf nearly shoved me underneath the bus. No idea who it was, as quite a mob got on. Irritated by the conductor, who said, when he collected my fare, "Ane o' these days ye'll dae yoursel' a mischief gin ye're sae precipitous." It was like being rebuked by an elder of the kirk. In fact, I bet that's what he is on Sundays. However, I know better than to argue with anybody in uniform in a foreign country, so I accepted my change and said nothing.

'Began the walk in fine, clear weather and was soon descending through woods — silver birch mostly — to the banks of a river called the Allander Water. The track followed the stream for a bit. You and Hera missed some very pleasant walking by joining The Way at Drymen instead of doing the whole stint.

'Up hill and away from the stream after that and got on to a piece of moorland which is one of Glasgow's playgrounds.

'Crossed the ridge and then had easy walking along a track which your guidebook informs me was once the drive up to a stately home. I went through more woods and came upon lots and lots of wild flowers. Am no botanist, but recognised yellow tormentil, heath bedstraw and scabious, but there were lots of others. Up to that point I had connected Scotland only with heather, harebells and cottongrass.

'After the numbers of people who had been on the path of moorland — really a wild sort of park — I seemed to have the woods to myself. Sat down with my back to one of the thickets and took your guidebook out of your rucksack to bone up on The Way. Talk about history repeating itself! I was reading the piece about the history of smugglers taking cover behind thickets in this very Mugdock Wood and having a bloody set-to with excisemen and soldiers when it damn well happened to *me*! Somebody must have been in that thicket behind me and must have crept out with the intention of belting me over the head. Luckily I heard a warning sound and I was able to wrench myself to one side, so most of the blow struck my arm and shoulder — though it did open up a nasty cut above my right eye.

'Whether the motive was robbery — and I can think of only one other — I don't know. If it was robbery, my assailant could have had no time to steal anything and not much chance anyway, because all my money was in a safety belt underneath my shirt and there was nothing much in the rucksack except a spare shirt and socks, soft shoes and some emergency rations. Of course I only know what I've been told since, but it appears that a party consisting of a doctor, his wife and two grown-up sons found me almost at once. I suppose the mugger heard them and made off. Fortunately, also, they were local people and knew that a nearby track led to the main road. To cut the story short, especially as I have it only by hearsay, I found myself in hospital with the devil of a headache and a very stiff arm and shoulder, but apparently nothing worse.

'I have had no chance to thank the doctor and his family. Having got me to hospital, they resumed their holiday or their day out, I suppose, and of course I shouldn't recognise them if, by any chance, I ever met them again, for I never saw them properly because of the blood which was running into my eyes from the head wound. The doctor at the hospital told me the family were called McKillop, but that's all I know.

'*Saturday*. Discharged myself from hospital, as feel much better and don't want to waste my holiday. Find myself reluctant to rejoin The Way, however, unless I can find at least one other person to accompany me. However, I have a powerful urge to find that stone building where you thought you found Carbridge's body, so I have hired a car and a driver.

'*Sunday*. Am in the Kingshouse hotel. All the rest of my news when I see you next Thursday. Don't know whether a post goes out from here today, but you should get this, with any luck, before I arrive.'

Hera was already home again. She had gone off on the Monday before Sandy travelled north on the Wednesday. She looked so haggard and exhausted that I was quite concerned and asked her whether she had been whooping it up in Paris. She turned on me in a bad temper and said that, if Sandy and I would see reason and take her into the partnership, she could give up the modelling jobs and all the travelling they entailed. She was in no state to be argued with, so I advised her to take things easy for a bit. This was at the office, where she had dropped in to tell me she was back. I was worried and I sent my secretary home with her with instructions to see that she had something to eat, and then went to bed. Our Miss Moore (Elsa to Sandy and me) is both firm and sympathetic. In any case, a woman is far better at coping with another woman than ever a man can be.

'She is very tired and upset,' said Miss Moore upon her return to the office. 'She wanted to come in again tomorrow to help out while Alexander is away, but I told her that we had the Pallister contract to negotiate and her presence would only be a distraction, not a help.'

'I hope you convinced her,' I said. 'She has wasted quite enough of our time already. People can't come into a busy office and pick up the threads as though they were picking up dropped stitches in a piece of knitting.'

'That is a very clever way of putting it, Comrie.' (We all used first names in the office.)

'Yes,' I said. 'I'm a very brainy bloke when I make the effort.' Elsa and I had a very pleasant no-nonsense relationship and I valued it very much.

Exactly what she had said to Hera I do not know, but whatever it was it seemed to have been effective, for Hera did not show up again at the office. I went round to see her each evening. She seemed unusually subdued. I would have told her about the thuggish attack on Sandy, but as soon as he got back he had repeated his request that I should not mention it. Hera enquired whether I had heard about his holiday, so I thought the safest thing was to say that since his return he had talked of nothing much except the proposed visit to Stockholm. This, up to a point, was true, although I could not understand at the time why I was not to mention to Hera that he had been attacked by a mugger in the well-named Mugdock Wood. As it turned out, he had not felt well enough to search for the stone building.

He telephoned me from Stockholm, told me everything was going very nicely and asked after Hera. He had negotiated contracts for two of our authors and obviously was feeling pleased with himself. I asked how his injuries were getting on. He said his arm and shoulder were still badly bruised and rather stiff, but the head wound was not troubling him and a woman at the book fair had told him that it gave him a very romantic appearance and had asked whether it was the result of a duel.

I was very glad to see him back. I was having a sticky time with Hera, who had recovered her health but not her temper, and my lot was not being made easier by the publisher of one of our authors who wanted us to persuade the lady to agree to a

ten per cent royalty instead of the twelve and a half which she
claimed she had been promised by word of mouth in the publisher's office. She had nothing in writing, but stuck to her
story and negotiations (if the acrimonious exchanges could be
so called) were still going on when Sandy returned to the office
and sorted things out.

'Ten per cent and a slightly larger advance,' he said to our
author. 'I can get them to agree to that, I'm sure. After all,
Delia dear, a bird in the hand is worth two in the bush and
money in your bank account is better than looking for a pot of
gold at the end of a rainbow. Let's put down a few figures on a
bit of paper and then I'll take you out to lunch.'

'Thank God,' I said to him later, 'for the authors who *don't*
come to see us!'

'Oh, I don't know,' he said. 'I do feel that the personal touch
is important. Besides, she's not a bad old girl. As a matter of
fact, I'm quite sure she *really* thinks she was promised twelve
and a half.'

'Not on the first five thousand,' I said. 'Not on *her* sales!'

'She's industrious and keeps up her output. We don't want to
lose her.'

'*You* may not!' I said, remembering various passages at arms
we had had with the lady over a number of years.

'How is Hera?' he asked.

'Prickly. I wonder what happened when she took that trip to
Paris? I think something there must have upset her. Besides,
she's still brooding over our refusal to take her into partnership.
We thought she would kick up sooner or later, and she has.'

'I'm sorry about that, Comrie, but you agree it wouldn't do,
don't you? Within a week she'd be trying to boss the whole
show. We've always realised that, so we must both stand firm.'

'Oh, I'll hold the fort,' I said. 'It's becoming a war of attrition,
but I certainly shan't give in.'

He looked at his reflection in a picture which hung on the
office wall and touched the scar which ran down the right side
of his forehead. It still looked rather angry, I thought. Knowing
what I knew at that juncture, I ought to have recognised his

touching it as being a symbolic gesture, but on this occasion what Hera (talking unkindly about my predilection for stumbling over dead bodies) has called my 'ESP or whatever' gave me no help at all.

# 12
## Europa and the Bull

Sandy had been back for less than a week when we had a prospective client. He was a surprise item if ever there were such a thing, but before he presented himself we had another visitor. This was young Trickett. News of his arrival reached us by way of the usual channels. Briggs, our office boy, reported to Polly, the senior typist of what she proudly called her 'pool' — herself and two youngsters fresh from commercial college — that: 'There's a young guy in horn-rims and a dirty sweater wants to see Mr Melrose.'

Polly translated this to Elsa as: 'There's a kind of poet-type in jeans and a roll-neck pullover. He is asking for Mr Melrose. Says his name is Trickett.'

From Elsa came the amendment: 'A rather dingy literary llama — see Hilaire Belloc — wants an interview, Comrie. I don't remember anybody on the books named Lucius Trickett, so he can't be one of ours. Will you see him?' (All this lovely informality would have gone, I knew, if we had taken Hera into partnership.)

'Trickett? Oh, yes, I know him. Send him in,' I said.

'That's the student bloke, isn't it?' said Sandy. 'I'll leave him to you.' He went to his own office, taking Elsa with him, and Trickett came in.

'Awfully sorry to bother you in business hours,' he said, 'but it seemed better than calling at your flat. I say, you know, it's getting a bit much, you know.'

'Bingley?' I asked.

'Yes, indeed. Won't let us alone, you know. Now we've done the geology of The Way, we've got stacks of notes to collate and

specimens to label before term starts, and it's nothing but in-
terruptions and all this endless questioning and going over the
old ground time and time again. He has even got the Glasgow
police to chase up Perth. I had a letter this morning. As for poor
old Bull, they absolutely hound him. What's to be done,
Melrose?'

'Goodness knows.'

'And a fat lot of help *that* is! Sorry! Not your fault, I know,
but it really is too sickening. We've nowhere to get together
except at the hall of residence and there our work is continually
interrupted by this snooping copper.'

'The get-together,' I said, 'does it include Coral and Patsy?'

'Yes, of course.'

'Are they residents, then?'

'Of course not. It's the men's hall, but we need the two girls
because of working on the West Highland project. The warden
is in residence now, of course, and he shoos the girls out every
day as soon as we've all had tea.'

'He wasn't in residence at the time of the party, though.'

'No, he was still on vacation, but he's been in the house ever
since.'

'The hall, during term, was only for men,' I said, 'so the
women at the party would not have known about that passage
to the cloakroom.'

'Naturally not. We had permission for them to use the
warden's own accommodation on the first floor. Patsy and
Coral had been briefed beforehand and were to tell the other
women – Jane Minch and Miss Camden and Tansy and Rhoda
and the girls in the orchestra, you know – where to go if they
wanted to powder up.'

'I don't know why,' I said, 'but it had not occurred to me
that the hall was unknown territory to the women students.
One takes so much for granted in these days of girls invading
boys' public schools and infiltrating men's colleges at the uni-
versities.'

'I hardly think there are unisex dormitories, though,' said
Lucius Trickett. 'Anyway, you have it right with regard to our

present predicament. Except for Patsy and Coral, the women had never been on the premises before. There is a strict rule against parties at the halls of residence. The dances are always held at the poly itself. That's why everything is so sickening, because I had a hell of a job to get the warden to agree to the Highland Way party and now, although it was no fault of mine, I feel I've let him down. If the party had been only for poly people, he would never have given permission, but it was for the Highland lot and now an outsider has to go and get himself murdered. It really is too bad.'

I sympathised, but could offer no help. I had learned something, however, which had changed my views more than a little. Had it not been for the corpse in the ruins on Rannoch Moor, I would have thought that the stab in the back which had killed poor Carbridge was more of a woman's than a man's crime, but even though the Rannoch murder was known to have been committed by a man, that man was an habitual criminal and, to such, the ordinary rules of fair play do not apply. More than once, when I thought about the poly murder — and it was seldom out of my mind — I had considered the possibility of its having been committed by a woman. Now, however, Trickett appeared to have made that idea improbable. It seemed that only the men would have known where that dark passage was. The women concerned were likely to have been ignorant of the layout of the building.

I re-visualised what I myself knew of it. We had been admitted at the front door by Trickett himself and had been led straight past the main staircase to the common-room where the orchestra, consisting of several young men and three girls, was already assembled. We had been greeted by Patsy in all the erotic splendour of her Turkish get-up. The room had three doors, the one by which we had entered, the one I had opened to get out and smoke my cigarette and by which Coral and Freddie had brought in the relays of food, and a third door which I had been told led only to a small wing which housed the sick-bay and which was always kept locked unless one of the students was ill.

Bull, it was clear, had been stationed where I saw him so that he could answer any telephone calls, since the telephone would hardly have been audible anywhere else with so much noise going on in the common-room. There was bound to be a telephone in the warden's quarters, I assumed, but, at the time, the warden was not in residence.

So much for Bull's having been stationed where I found him and for Trickett's having opened the front door to the guests. It followed that the only woman who might know of the passage in which I had stumbled upon the body was Coral, who would have passed Bull's end of the passage when she and Freddie were rushing down Bull's corridor with the trays of food. It was in the highest degree unlikely, however, that she had enquired where the little passage led or even noticed it particularly, and equally unlikely that Freddie would have mentioned it to her considering that it led straight to the men's cloakroom.

I thought of the electric lightbulb which was missing. Bull had put off replacing it because to put in another one meant going and getting a ladder. I did not know where the ladder was kept, but I assumed that Detective-Inspector Bingley had long ago dealt with this point. Bull had been lax, of course, but that, in itself, was not a criminal offence.

Bull himself was certainly too short to have been able to remove or replace the bulb without a ladder, but he had been seated on an ordinary kitchen chair, so I wondered why it had not occurred to him to use that to stand on.

I considered the other men. Todd and Trickett were both tall enough to have reached the bulb without the aid of a ladder, and, although they both topped me, I too was tall enough to have reached it, and so, come to that, was Carbridge himself, who was just about my own height. The puzzle which nobody had solved was how and why Carbridge had been in the house before the party was due to begin. He was not an ex-poly man, so would not have known automatically of the basement entrance left open for the students. I wondered who had put him wise or had brought him there so early.

I wondered how much strength it took to plunge a knife into

a man's heart. Todd, I assumed, would have had no difficulty and, although Trickett was a string-bean of a fellow, he was wiry and tough and might have put on a lot of muscle by dint of his delving and chipping on the tour in Scotland. This might even apply to the female geologists, too. They had appeared to be working even harder than the men when Hera and I saw them at it.

There remained Andrew Perth, but by that time there was little doubt that Bingley and the Glasgow police could account for his movements during the period under review. There was the question of alibis for the rest of us. On the day of the party, provided that the doctors had estimated the time of death more or less correctly, Hera and I were able to provide alibis for one another irrespective of shop girls, cinema attendants and all the rest of it, so long as the police were prepared to take the word of an engaged couple. All the same, I still hoped that nobody had mentioned to Bingley the punch-up I had had with Carbridge at Crianlarich.

It was at this point in my meditations that our unexpected client arrived and was announced by the hierarchy in ascending order of importance thus:

*Briggs to Polly:* 'Little old geezer stinking of mothballs in his best suit wants to see Mr Melrose.'
*Polly to Elsa:* 'Something off the shop floor called Bull is asking for Mr Melrose and won't be happy till he gets him.'
*Elsa to me:* 'There's a Mr Bull, Comrie. Seems harmless, but may have a bomb concealed on his person.'
(*Trickett:* 'Oh, well, I'll be going. Do what you can for Bull, won't you?')
*Me:* 'Show the visitor in. Goodbye, then, Lucius.'
*Elsa (when Trickett had gone):* 'I don't know where you pick them up, but it's your choice.'

Our visitor was Bull. He was impressed by his reception, it appeared, but slightly morose about it.

'It's as bad as tryin' to get into Buck'nam Palace without an invite,' he said, 'though that's been done, too, I berlieve.'

'I know. Never mind. Take a seat. Any news?'

'Not of the kind you means. That dick is still measurin' out my footprints, so to say. I can't get him off my back no-how. But that's not what I come about.'

'I can't give you a job here, I'm afraid.'

'You can and you can't. Any road, young Trickett said come to you, so I've come.'

'Trickett? So that's what he came about! Say on!'

'I wants to write me life story.'

'That sounds a tall order.'

'So it would be if I was to do your actual writin', but that 'ud be beyond me. I've forgot most of the schoolin' I ever had. So I goes to the Citizens' Advice, see, and puts it to 'em and there was a young feller there seemed interested and he says, quite serious-like, "What you need is a ghost," he says. I thinks he's havin' me on, but no.'

'No, he wasn't having you on,' I agreed. 'It's often done. One party supplies the information and the other party — usually a trained journalist — writes it up and takes a share of the proceeds or else is paid for his work by the principal in the undertaking.'

'Right. So, not knowin' no one, I asks young Trickett and he advises me to come to you to see what chance I got and to pave the way, like.'

'Not a lot of chance of publication, I'm afraid,' I said regretfully. 'You see, Bull, autobiographies and biographies have to be about well-known people whom other people are interested in.'

'Wouldn't they be interested in a hangman's deperty assistant? There's plenty in favour of bringin' back the rope, you know.'

'But you can't mean — '

'Oh, yes, and better nor that. Went back to me real name, of course, when I took the job at the hall of residence. The warden knows me personal history, but nobody else. Lost me position, you see, never mind why; it will all be in the book. I didn't fancy comin' down to bein' a screw at Parkhurst or Dartmoor or wherever it would have been. Me life wouldn't have been worth a dog-biscuit among a buggerin' lot of bloody murderers, specially with a name like mine.'

'You astound me, Bull, you really do! The only thing is that I'm pretty sure it's been done already, you know — this auto-biography of a public executioner.'

'Oo by?'

'I couldn't say off-hand.'

'So nor couldn't nobody else, then, could 'em? Look, supposin' as how whoever it is and me gets the book wrote up and put in typin', what's the chance you'll take it on and see it through for us?'

'It would depend entirely upon how good a book it was, and I warn you that our standards are high. We're not in the market for duds. We have our reputation to consider. Look here, I'll tell you what I'll do. If I can find you a reputable "ghost", I'll let you know; and if *we* recommend a ghost-writer, it will be a good one. I would have to arrange a meeting, though, to make sure that the journalist is willing to take the job on. I've got somebody in mind, as a matter of fact, but I'm not sure that yours is a job which would appeal to a woman.'

'Fair enough,' he said. 'Thanks, Mr Melrose. Be seein' you. Thought you might be interested.'

'All right, Bull. I'll look into it. By the way, what makes you think that, when hanging was done away with, they would make you a screw at one of HM prisons?'

'Why wouldn't they? I'd given good service, hadn't I? Got testimonials, haven't I, for all they're writ in a foreign lang-widge.'

'I shouldn't have thought you were tall enough to take a job as a prison warder. You weren't tall enough to put that electric lightbulb back without a ladder, were you?'

I could see he thought the reference to the past was rather tactless. As soon as he had gone, I called in Sandy and Elsa. When Elsa had finished laughing, she said, 'Why don't you kill two birds with one stone?'

'As how?'

'Stick him on to Dame Beatrice's granddaughter and so get your psychiatrist interested in Carbridge's murder from a personal standpoint. We've got Miss Lestrange's name on our books. She has published a couple of novels, but they didn't do much good, so she trained as a journalist and works on her local paper. Now and again she gets a piece accepted by the Sunday papers and women's mags, and she does quite a bit of ghosting. She is down under the Stone House address, but that is given merely to inspire confidence and impress Sally's clients. I don't suppose Dame Beatrice has anything to do with it except to give permission for her address to be used. I expect her secretary is told to re-address any letters which come for the granddaughter and send them on. It's just a family thing. Blood is thicker than water, after all.'

'Oh, well,' I said, 'the connection with Dame Beatrice makes my job easier in a way. I shall ring up and ask where I can get in touch with Sally Lestrange and explain why I want to see her. Of course there isn't the slightest chance that we shall sponsor Bull's book and attempt to wish it on to a publisher.'

'Why not?' said Elsa. 'Mycroft and Holmes might take it if it's any good at all. They specialise in that sort of thing.'

'Anyway, I'll ring up and find out what's doing,' I said. 'Obviously the Stone House is only an accommodation address, as you say. I suppose Miss Lestrange's own isn't very impressive.'

I rang up at four. As the song says, everything stops for tea. Laura answered, so I told her why I was calling the Stone House and asked where I could get in touch with Miss Sally Lestrange.

'Hang on a minute,' she said. The next voice was that of Dame Beatrice, so I explained myself again to her.

'How enterprising people are!' she said. 'A hangman's assistant, you say. I wish you would come and see me, Mr Melrose, before you tackle Sally. To quote Oberon — unless Shakespeare was making it all up — "this falls out better than I could devise". When may we expect you?'

'Whenever is convenient to you.'

'Come to lunch tomorrow, then.'

'Thank you very much.'

So, once again, I found myself at the Stone House. Before lunch, Laura gave me Miss Lestrange's address and after lunch we sat in the garden in upholstered cane chairs — deck chairs are

one of my abominations — and talked about Bull and the death
of Carbridge.

I referred to the complaints of Trickett and Bull that they
were still being harassed by Bingley and I also mentioned that,
if Carbridge had been dead for at least four hours when the
police surgeon first looked at the body, he must have been on
the premises at four in the afternoon or earlier. 'And I can't
think why,' I said.

'I wonder how long the students took in the preparation of
their party,' said Laura. 'An hour, two hours, three?'

'Not more than two at the very outside, I should say. It wasn't
like Christmas, for example. I mean, there were no decorations
to put up, no elaborate cooking to be done. So far as I could
see, the food was nothing but hamburgers, cocktail sausages,
potato crisps and salted peanuts. There was nothing which
could not be handed round more or less on the spot. There were
mugs and glasses set out, but that could have been done in less
than ten minutes and all the drinks were in bottles, so there was
no preparation needed there.'

'In any case, as one of the invited guests, Mr Carbridge would
hardly have been asked for help in getting the party ready,'
said Dame Beatrice.

'I still don't know how he found out how to oil into the place
without anybody else's knowledge. I suppose he may have
heard the students mention the back entrance at one of the
youth hostels and simply stored up the information. He could
even have arranged to meet one of the students there, but it
would need to be early on, because later the other students
would be getting the party ready.'

'You mean *cherchez la femme*, then,' said Laura.

'But *les femmes* knew nothing about the geography of the
hall of residence. It's a pad for men students,' I said. Laura
laughed and said that she had been a student, too, in her time.
'Not that we went in for present-day capers,' she added, 'but
there was a men's college not so far from ours and bets of
various kinds were offered and, from time to time, accepted.
Besides, if Carbridge wanted to meet one of the girls and couldn't

meet her at his digs for some reason, what was to prevent him
from sending her a note and suggesting they met at the back
door of the hall and he would take her in with him?'

'I think it must have been the other way round, if it happened
at all,' said Dame Beatrice. 'I think your reconstruction is un-
arguable, but, as you have indicated, the women students probably knew more about the men's hall of residence than the
authorities may have thought suitable. Therefore it is more
likely that the assignation was made by the girl than by Mr
Carbridge. Had it been suggested by him, she might or might
not have agreed to it.'

'She wouldn't, if we're talking about Patsy Carlow,' I put in.
'Todd was interested in her, too, or so I was told, and anybody
who could have Todd wasn't very likely to bother about an ass
like Carbridge. I even had to keep an eye on Todd and Hera, if
you want to know.'

'The plot thickens,' said Laura. 'Suppose Patsy makes the
ploy, Carbridge is flattered and goes blithely to his doom?'

'Oh, no, of course he — I mean, I'm sure Patsy didn't do anything of the sort,' I said. 'Why should she? Carbridge was pretty
frightful in a back-slapping, "old boy, old boy" sort of way, and
a bit of a nuisance to women, perhaps, but he was utterly harmless, I'm sure. If he was lured into that house and murdered, it
had nothing to do with young Patsy Carlow. She is as silly as a
wench can be, but — '

'Then you mean somebody sent Carbridge a note in her
name,' said Laura, 'and he fell into the trap.'

'Dear me!' said Dame Beatrice. 'No wonder Sally's novels
had so little success with the public! Her plots must have been
singularly inadequate. Let us hope the story told by the hangman's hanger-on will prove more profitable to her.'

'Is there any chance that this Bull's reminiscences *will* get
published?' asked Laura. I replied that I would have no idea
until I had read them, but that our secretary, a knowledgeable
young woman, thought there might be a hope.

'It depends upon what Miss Lestrange can do with the material and, of course, how much of it the old chap can supply,' I

said. 'People who don't know the ropes have no idea how much and what kind of information is needed to make a full-length book. Personally, knowing what I do about Bull, I doubt very much whether Miss Lestrange will find the job worth her while. All the famous murderers have been done to death — well, I don't quite mean that. I mean, they've been written up and their crimes dissected and their trials analysed and goodness knows what-all. I can't imagine that Bull will have anything fresh to say and, in any case, he was hardly a principal figure, I gather.'

'I don't know how they could ever find anybody willing to hang another person,' said Laura, 'but I believe I would have hated even more to be the judge who had to pass sentence, than I would to be the hangman.'

'Both are in the hands of a higher power, to wit, the jury,' I said. 'It is the twelve good persons and true with whom the verdict of innocent or guilty rests. The judge merely passes sentence and the hangman merely used to carry it out. Personally I would rather be hanged than serve a life sentence. I'm very sure of that.'

'You say that now, but only because you are in no danger of either,' said Laura. 'You might feel differently if you were in the condemned cell.'

'The trouble with juries,' said Dame Beatrice, 'is that they have no conception of what really constitutes evidence. If they had, I, for one, should not be with you today.'

I stared at her, but she cackled, so I concluded that she had not meant what her sinister hint implied. Anyway, I had found out what I wanted to know. Because of the connection Sally had formed with my agency, Dame Beatrice was prepared to take an active part in solving the mystery of Carbridge's death.

# 13

## *Suggestions for a Replay*

It was Laura who kept the ball rolling. 'It's a long time since we saw much of Sally,' she said. 'She has popped in for an occasional lunch, but she hasn't stayed here since you both went to Sir Humphry Calshott's house and she let herself in for hunting a Loch Ness monster at Tannasgan. Do you remember?'

'It is not an experience to be forgotten,' said Dame Beatrice, 'and, when it was over, Sir Humphry (against his better judgement, I suspect) published Sally's first novel. Time passes like an ever-rolling stream, but the flotsam it leaves behind stays with us. I wonder what arrangements can be made for Sally and Mr Bull to get together over this autobiography?'

'I think there is only one course open to them,' I said. 'Miss Lestrange is a free agent; Bull is not. It looks to me as though she will have to go to the hall of residence to jot down his reminiscences if she takes on the job. Once term starts, Bull won't be able to get away from his duties and he lives in.'

'And all those wild-eyed, frenzied male polytechnic students will be back,' said Laura. 'The girl must be chaperoned.'

'Exactly,' said Dame Beatrice, leering at her secretary.

'Ah!' I said. 'So that's it, is it? Well, I'm delighted to hear it. It's high time someone with an open mind investigated the circumstances of Carbridge's death.'

'I had the impression you didn't like him much,' said Laura.

'It's because of that.'

'What do you mean?'

'Well, the police never really had anything on Bull, and Bingley knew it. He only arrested him as a gesture. Now he's got

to find somebody else to stick the label on. As soon as somebody — probably under pressure — blows the gaff and tells him
I knocked Carbridge for six at Crianlarich, I'm in the cart.'

'Yes,' said Dame Beatrice, 'you had attacked him. You
probably had the best of reasons, but those will not weight the
scales of justice in your favour; you were present at the students'
party and it was you who found the body.'

'I have an alibi from the midday onwards. Carbridge must
have been dead long before Hera and I showed up at the party.
We shopped, had a late lunch together and went to a cinema.
I'm sure I can prove all this. Besides, until I was told of the unlocked back door, the students' entrance to the hall of residence,
I knew nothing about how to get into the house except by
ringing the front-door bell.'

'What?' said Laura. 'That plea won't hold water. Oh, not that
I don't believe you, but the police will argue that you could
have heard about a way in by a back door from the students
who walked The Way with you. They'll say they don't remember
talking about it, but things do come out in conversation and
seem so trivial at the time that nobody takes any notice unless
something blows up later.'

'Where, in London, is the hall of residence to be found?'
asked Dame Beatrice. I gave her the address and Laura wrote it
down. She said that she would get in touch with the warden. 'I
take your point about the autobiography,' she said. 'As
Mahomet cannot, by reason of his occupation, go to the mountain, Sally must go to Mahomet. But I shall see to it that she
does not go alone.'

'Sally would hardly relish being called a mountain,' said
Laura. 'I wonder what the warden thinks about this autobiography business?'

'I wonder how much he knows about the whole project,' I
said.

Next morning at the office Sandy spoke to me on a subject
which had crossed my own mind more than once, but which,
because of Hera, I had never raised. He came into my room,
waited while I finished dictating a letter to Elsa, gave her some

envelopes and said, 'I've looked through this lot and some of it needs a woman's tactful approach. Tell Minster and Wynn that, if they think Tacitus Player will agree to staying on the same advance for his next three books, they've got another think coming; and, if Latter and Day don't pay up soon on that textbook they commissioned from Seppie Leveret, proceedings are jolly well going to be taken which will make them as sick as mud. Put it all in your own winsome way, dear. We don't want any hard feelings. All the same, tell M. and W. that Player can sell his stuff anywhere nowadays, and that if they don't want him on their list there's plenty as does. As for Seppie Leveret, the poor woman has been an angel of patience. She spent two years writing that damn book for them and she has to eat and clothe herself and keep the home fires burning, just like the rest of us. Sock it to them good and proper, but always the kid glove, not the iron gauntlet, on the hand which manipulates the hosepipe.'

'Don't he talk lovely!' said Elsa. She blew him a kiss and went out, taking her sheaves with her. Sandy waved me to a chair, went to a cupboard and took out bottles and glasses.

'Those letters will keep her busy for a bit,' he said. 'I wanted to get her out of the way. Comrie, don't you think it's time we offered that girl a partnership?'

'I think it is. I've thought so for a long while. Anchor her down, you mean.'

'Oh, I didn't know she'd had offers to leave us.'

'Lord, yes. She told Hera so when she took Hera home the other day, and Hera told *me*. She thought it was a plank in her platform and said as much. She said that, if Elsa went, there would be a hole which she herself could fill.'

'Did she say that to Elsa?'

'I shouldn't think so.'

'It isn't like Elsa to talk about her own affairs.'

'Oh, you know what women are. Even the best of them, given the chance to let their back hair down, will let it toss in the wind like the mane of Odin's horse.'

'I don't believe Elsa would. If you don't mind my saying so, I think Hera made the whole thing up.'

'Quite possibly. You can see what a spot I'm going to be in, though, if we *do* make Elsa a partner. I'm all for it, mind you, but I'm in for a pretty rough time when it happens.'

'Still, fair's fair. She didn't tell Hera about any offers she's had, I'm certain of that. Her whole training is geared to her never talking out of turn. All the same, I'm prepared to bet that she *has* had offers and, human nature being what it is, one of those offers has only got to be *big* enough, if you see what I mean — '

'Perfectly. Right, then, let's go ahead. That's what I meant when I talked of getting Elsa anchored here. We can't afford to lose her.'

'What about the name of the firm? Won't she expect to have hers added to ours?'

'Not at first, anyhow. I like the name Alexander Comrie and don't want it altered. We could make that a condition, I think, but she'll probably see for herself the point of keeping the name we're known by. She's a very sensible girl.'

So Elsa, obviously delighted, was added to the managerial strength and was adamant that the name of the firm should not be changed.

'It wouldn't inspire confidence,' she said. 'Alexander Comrie has such a nice, solid, *Scottish* sound about it and it's known and respected all over the place.' So Alexander Comrie we remained and all was gas and gaiters until Hera found out that we had made Elsa a full partner and that her name, although not in our trade title, was on our stationery.

'What's all this, and since when?' she demanded one evening. She was spending the evening at my flat and turning it upside down as usual on one of her tidying-up blitzes.

'What's that?'

She had been tidying the shelves in my wardrobe — an operation I thought completely unnecessary, but one which she insisted upon carrying out from time to time, and had come upon a piece of paper on which I had scribbled down a list of things for my charwoman to send to the laundry. I had meant

to copy the list on the official card the laundry always en-
closed in the package when the washing came home, but had
procrastinated.

'What's this on the agency's notepaper?' She came towards
me and held out the scribbled-on sheet. I took it and looked it
over.

'Only a tentative laundry list,' I said, as off-handedly as I
could.

'I can see that. You haven't altered the trade name, but
what is Elsa Moore's name doing after Sandy's full name and
yours?'

'You would hardly expect it to come in front of ours, would
you?'

'Oh, don't hedge! You've made her a partner and I want an
explanation.'

'No explanation is due to you, my dear girl. If I had appeared
at your flat with lipstick on my face, or if, in this quite unnecessary tidying-up which you know I hate, you had found a
girl's pants which you knew were not yours, you might be in
order in asking certain questions, but what is on our official
notepaper is our business, Sandy's and mine, not yours.'

'So that's it! You *have* made her a partner!'

'Yes, of course that's it. Elsa has been with us and served the
firm wonderfully well for more than five years. We decided to
give some slight recognition to that fact, that is all. And now,
for heaven's sake, stop messing about with my shirts and ties
and let's have a drink.'

I folded the piece of paper, put it in my pocket and waited
for the next outburst, but all she said was 'You'll be sorry for
this.'

'I *am* sorry — sorry that you found the laundry list, if you
don't like its printed heading. As a matter of fact, it was
Sandy's suggestion that we should let Elsa in and put her name
on our notepaper, but, of course, I agreed. It is only to safe-
guard ourselves.'

'Against what?'

'Against losing her to another firm, of course. You know

there was always the danger of that.'

'Oh, yes? And you have never seen me as an efficient sub-stitute? Oh, well!'

She accepted a drink in her usual graceful way and the only further reference she made to the unfortunate laundry list was to tell me to include the loose covers on the two armchairs in the bedroom. She left earlier than usual and, although I saw her home, she did not suggest that I should go in, so I knew that we had not finished with the subject of Elsa and the partnership.

Sally Lestrange turned up at the office two days later. She had made an appointment over the telephone and was received by Elsa and passed on to me. She was a pleasantly direct and business-like young woman and came to the point at once.

'What are the chances of publication?' she asked. 'I don't want to spend a lot of time on something which is never going to see the light of day. I've made that clear to Bull.'

'As I told the man himself, it depends upon the material and upon how it's handled. You know as much about that sort of thing as I do,' I said.

'Yes, but the material itself. I've talked to Bull and I can't believe he's got much to offer.'

'Then turn him down.'

'My grandmother would be disappointed if I did. No, I must carry on, I think. I just wondered what chance the thing might have.'

'I'll tell you what chance it *could* have,' I said, struck by a sudden inspiration. 'Make it clinical.'

'Make it what?'

'Turn it into a case history. Let Bull tell his story in his own way. Don't sub-edit. Take him down *verbatim* if your shorthand will stand the strain of his vowels and elisions and then get Dame Beatrice to write an introduction to the book as a study of the psychology of a hangman's assistant. Bull will be tre-mendously flattered and if she will do it we shall achieve publication all right. Some of her views are refreshingly un-orthodox and will provoke controversy not only among the *cognoscenti*, but in the popular press.'

'A bestseller!' breathed Miss Lestrange.

'Don't count the chickens, of course, but at any rate, if you can get Dame Beatrice to agree, there will be no doubt about publication.'

'She *will* agree. She wants to get in on this murder which seems to have happened where Bull lives and works. He tells me that it was this murder which sparked off the idea that he should write his memoirs. One thing does lead to another, doesn't it?'

She was right enough there. The thing which led to another in my case was the new partnership. My private correspondence, delivered at my flat a couple of days later, included a registered packet which contained the engagement ring I had put on Hera's finger some months earlier. It was her answer to the appointment of Elsa to our board of directors, as Sandy now grandly termed it.

I was not unduly disturbed. I was sorry that Hera was taking the matter so much to heart, but I had expected a vigorous reaction. It had come, so that was a relief. Besides, I felt that she would have second thoughts when she had had time to cool off. I felt sure that, when she had had a chance to think things over, she would have sense enough to realise that, if we were going to admit anybody to partnership, Elsa was the obvious choice. She had the knowledge and the experience. Besides, not only Sandy and myself, but the rest of the staff got on well with her. She was hardworking and conscientious and, better than that, she had *flair*, a wonderful way with difficult authors and a grand sense of humour.

I wrote in brief acknowledgement of the registered package and ended the letter *'Love, C.'* I posted it on my way to the office and told Sandy about it when I got there. He expressed concern, but I said I was sure she would come round when she had thought matters over.

'She was dead nuts on coming in with us, of course,' I said. 'Perhaps we ought to have waited a bit before we co-opted Elsa.'

'Oh, I don't think so,' said Sandy. 'We might have lost Elsa if we'd waited much longer.'

That morning Polly brought my coffee.

'To what are we indebted?' I asked, as she set down my cup. Usually one of the juniors brought it.

'That pullover-and-jeans is here again,' she replied, 'and Miss Moore has got an author.' She made it sound as though Elsa was suffering from a sick headache and, knowing some of our authors, I thought it more than likely that this was so. 'Anyway, it's you he wants to see,' Polly went on, 'so I told him I'd find out. You drink that coffee and let him wait.'

'You might possibly give him a cup, too. It will help him pass the time,' I suggested.

'Do you know what fresh-ground coffee costs these days?' she asked tartly. 'Still, all right, if you say so.'

'It will be a treat for the poor boy,' I said. 'Surely your motherly heart goes out to him?'

'I don't like young men in horn-rims.'

'That is mere prejudice.'

'He dresses like a tramp that's lost all self-respect, and yet if those horn-rims cost a penny under sixty pounds I should be surprised. It's what they call inverted snobbery.'

'He's a student of geology.'

'No wonder he looks so grubby.' She waited while I drank my coffee, then she took away the cup and added, 'Shall I send him in?'

'Yes, when he's finished the coffee you are going to give him. You might add a couple of substantial biscuits. I expect he's hungry. Boys always are.'

When Trickett came in, he was obviously the bearer of tidings. His thin face was flushed and his spectacles glittered. He reminded me of Gussie Fink-Nottle contemplating a particularly fine collection of newts.

'I say, you know,' he said, 'we've had a Visitation, you know.'

'Come, come!' I said. 'The time of the final apocalypse is not yet. I suppose you mean Dame Beatrice Lestrange Bradley has shown up at the hall of residence.'

This deflated him. He took a chair and said in disappointed tones, 'Oh, you knew. Yes, she turned up with the woman who is going to write up Bull's life story. The warden has given full permission to them both and is all over the old lady. He's already arranged for her to give a talk to the students when term starts. It seems she is very well known in her own circles, but she's not going to talk on her own subject. She's going to talk about murder.'

'Well, that *is* her subject — a subsidiary one, perhaps, but, nevertheless, her own. She is a noted criminologist and murderers are her speciality.'

'I say, that's fine! Everybody loves a good murder. The rest of the poly lot will be as envious as Cassius when they know we've actually been mixed up in one.'

'They probably know already. The story has been in all the papers.'

'Still, the walkers and the orchestra were the only ones of our lot who were actually there when it happened. Dame Beatrice is fearfully interested. She wants to find out how we all reacted and will add what we tell her to round out her talk. We're going to have another party before she gives her talk, but she's giving it herself. She wants me to give out most of the invitations, though. It's to be held at a restaurant where they will give us a private room — La Carpe Heureuse. Do you know it?'

'Yes. I've taken Hera there several times. Marvellous food.'

'Ah, Miss Camden, yes. Do you think she will come? Todd is invited, too, of course. He took Patsy Carlow to a nightclub the other evening, as term hasn't started yet, and Miss Camden and Freddie Brown were invited as well. I suppose their job was to keep the party clean. Patsy is only too apt to step high, wide and plentiful if anybody treats her to champagne. She told Coral she had bedded down with Todd, but Coral says that was only wishful thinking. Will you pass the invitation on to Miss Camden? Six thirty on Wednesday for seven. Black ties or a dark suit. The warden and his wife are coming.'

'Is Detective-Inspector Bingley to be one of the company?' I asked facetiously.

'I shouldn't think so. He would rather cramp our style, don't you think?' said Trickett seriously.

'What about Bull, who is on the threshold of becoming a bestselling author?'

'Poor old Bull! No, he won't be there, but Dame Beatrice is bringing Miss Lestrange and Mrs Gavin.'

'Mrs Gavin? — oh, of course, Laura!'

'They wondered whether your partner would like to come — Mr Alexander, isn't it?'

'Storey, actually. We combine our first names for business purposes. Yes, I think he would very much like to come. Are the members of the orchestra invited?'

'Dame Beatrice has left it to me, so I think not. Ostensibly the thing is my party, so I've decided that the only poly people will be those who went on the walk. Dame Beatrice particularly wants Perth to come and has sent him a return ticket and will book him in for Wednesday night at an hotel. Well, with our people, including you and Todd and Miss Camden, the warden and his wife, Miss Lestrange, Mrs Gavin and Dame Beatrice herself, we shall be quite a large enough gathering, I think. I say, who is the stunning young woman who looks like the Queen of Sheba and makes me feel as though I'm six years old and have jam on my face?'

'Our junior partner, Miss Elsa Moore.'

'Is she Jewish?'

'Irish, I would have thought.'

'I bet she had a Jewish mother, then. You can't mistake the arrogance of that type of Jewish girl, you know, when they're as good-looking as that and so damned brainy with it.'

'Good gracious, Elsa isn't arrogant! Far from it. She's the quietest, most amenable person.'

'All the same,' he said, 'I bet she ties your authors up in knots if they come here looking for an argument. I say! You wouldn't like to bring her to the party, would you? I can invite anybody I like, you know, and I do admire Miss Moore most awfully.'

'I can't bring Elsa if Hera is going to be there.'

'Ah,' he said, taking off the horn-rims which Polly had criticised and gesturing with them at me. 'Like that, is it?'

'Just like that, but not for the reason you seem to think,' I said. He smiled pityingly and shook his head.

# 14

## Not an Official Enquiry

As though nothing had happened to separate us, I rang up Hera, told her about the invitation and asked whether she was prepared to accept it. She replied in the same liberal spirit and said that she would look forward to the gathering.

'Pick me up half an hour before you had intended to,' she said, 'and I'll give you a drink. What is the party in aid of, anyway?'

'I think Dame Beatrice wants to size us all up.'

'Good gracious! What an uncomfortable thought! Never mind. When do I expect you on Wednesday?'

'Would a quarter to six be all right?'

When we met, it was like old times. She was wearing a dinner dress of midnight blue and looked more beautiful than ever. I told her so. Neither of us referred to the return of the engagement ring. I had it with me, but, unless the right moment offered itself, there was no point in attempting to return it.

At six fifteen I called a taxi and we arrived at the restaurant to find more than half the company already assembled and chattering over cocktails in an anteroom to that in which we were to dine. Cheerfulness was the keynote and, needless to say, Carbridge was never mentioned. The students (Patsy in a surprisingly simple and restrained dark green dress which she informed me she had borrowed for the occasion because the warden was going to be present) all had best-behaviour faces and sleekly groomed hair. Dame Beatrice was in dark red and the warden's wife in black and gold, but to my mind the lovely Hera stole the picture; there was no doubt that Todd thought so too, and, as a fair-minded man, I could not blame him for wanting to dance attendance on her.

I had calculated that, if everybody whom Trickett had intended to invite had accepted, we should be seventeen at table, but there was an extra guest in the person of the warden's son, Dominic Terrance, an engaging youth who was going up to Cambridge as soon as the term started.

The dinner was *table d'hôte*, there was a choice of red or white wine and there were place cards, so that everybody knew where to sit. The seating had been worked out carefully, I thought. Dame Beatrice took the head of the table, Laura the foot, so that both of them had the rest of us in their eye. My dinner partner was Jane Minch and on my other side was Rhoda Green.

The warden and Mrs Terrance were on either side of Dame Beatrice and young Dominic partnered Tansy Parks. Sandy had refused the invitation without having given me any specific reason except to say that he was not acquainted with any of the company.

'You know Hera, me, Trickett, Sally Lestrange and Dame Beatrice,' I pointed out. He replied that he knew Dame Beatrice only by repute and that when Trickett had come to the office it was only to speak to me and not to him. He added that dinner parties which numbered more than four people were not much in his line unless all the guests were of the male sex, and that he could see Hera and myself any time he wished and in much less boring circumstances.

Conversation at table was lively and of a general nature, even Rhoda and Tansy joining in. Most of the subject matter was centred on the West Highland Way and, needless to say, again nobody mentioned Carbridge. When we rose from table, Todd said to me, 'I've been told that some of you are to go back with the warden, so I'll see Hera home. There'll be no hanky-panky. I know her too well for that.'

I found this remark disquieting, but there was no opportunity to question it. The students, delighted with their evening, were leaving and taxis were being summoned for the rest of us. Hera and Todd went off in the first one and I found myself in the vestibule of the restaurant with Dame Beatrice, Laura, Sally, Perth, young Dominic, the warden and his wife.

The Minches had gone off together on foot, so had Rhoda and Tansy, and the four students also appeared to be hunting in couples, for I saw Trickett and Coral go off in one direction and Freddie and Patsy in another.

I shared a taxi with Sally and Laura, while Dame Beatrice was accompanied by the warden and his wife and son, but, before the taxis came, Laura contrived to segregate me from the others.

'I expect you wonder what all this is about,' she said.

'Not at all. I think you and Dame Beatrice wanted to see all of our walking party together, so that you could sum up one against the other, so to speak. I don't know, though, why Perth and I have been invited to finish the evening at the hall of residence as guests of Mr and Mrs Terrance.'

'You may not know, but there is no harm in hazarding a guess.'

'In that case,' I said, 'perhaps Dame Beatrice is going to question Perth about the various relationships between members of the tour party and wants to have me present as a check on what he tells her.'

'That's about the size of it.'

When we reached the hall of residence, we were taken up to the warden's quarters. Having seen us settled and indicated a small side table which held bottles and glasses, he and his wife and son took themselves off, having told us that they would be in the small sitting-room next door. They took Sally with them. I poured whisky for myself, Perth and Laura, but Dame Beatrice refused a drink and, eyeing us benevolently, began her interrogation.

It was directed, as I had anticipated, at Perth, and I guessed from his demeanour that he had expected to be the leading light and was quite happy to be in that position. In his quiet way, and like most Scotsmen, he had a pretty good conceit of himself. Laura had produced writing materials from somewhere and was poised to record in shorthand what he had to say.

'You, my dear Mr Melrose,' Dame Beatrice said to me, 'will amend, confirm or contradict Mr Perth's statements if and when you see occasion to do so.'

'Aye,' said Perth approvingly, 'ye should always monitor your experiments. What is your wish that I should tell ye, mistress?'

'What different connotations the same word can have!' said Dame Beatrice. ' "Mistress" is a case in point. In England it means either a female employer of domestic servants or an alternative to a wife. In Scotland it is a form of address to a married woman of reputedly acceptable behaviour. I believe that the Scots' use of the word is in accordance with its original meaning, and is preferable, in my opinion, to the Frenchified and somewhat stilted "madam".'

'Mistress is used by Shakespeare in a pleasant way in *The Merry Wives of Windsor*,' said Laura. ' "Mistress Ford and Mistress Page are the liveliest of women." '

'Ladies of unblemished virtue and of great wit and charm,' I said, and I was about to recount my grandfather's reminiscences of his falling in love with Edith Evans in 1925 on seeing her as Mistress Page, when I realised that, as P.G.W. causes one of his characters to say, we are not put into this world for pleasure alone, so I left the little story untold and waited upon Dame Beatrice's next words.

'What did you make of Mr Carbridge?' she asked Perth. 'What was your first impression of him? Did you find reason to alter it in any way as the tour progressed?'

'I'll answer ye categorically. I thought the man was a fule when first I met him and I still think the man was a fule.'

'Interesting. Why did you think that, I wonder?'

'Ye have an English saying that onlookers see most of the game. I kept yon man Carbridge in my sights from the beginning.'

'Why?'

'There are types I dinna trust. Hot gospellers, practical jokers, do-gooders and "friends of a' the world" such as Carbridge. Leddy, I'm telling ye, that man was more sociable than a plague o' gnats.'

'Then why do you think he was killed? Gregariousness is not usually an incitement to murder.'

'Gin it willna weary the company or, maybe, gie great offence to Mr Melrose here, I could furnish ye wi' chapter and vairse.'

'Don't mind me,' I said. 'I suppose Hera comes into it somewhere, but I know you to be a gentleman, so anything you say will not come amiss so far as I am concerned. As a matter of fact, she has broken our engagement.'

'Och, the pity of it! Weel, mistress, I'll gie ye a potted vairsion o' the tour as I saw it, and ye may draw your ain conclusions.'

He proceeded to furnish us with details. In a sense, little that he said was new to me so far as the occasions on which Hera and I had been with the rest of the party were concerned, but, of course, for most of the time we had been on our own. He began by describing the meeting at the Glasgow youth hostel. Looking at me, he said that in his opinion Hera and Todd were old acquaintances, and apologetically he asked whether this piece of information came as a complete surprise to me.

'It certainly does,' I said. 'So far as I am aware, their previous meetings were the most casual and accidental encounters. They met in the corridor of the train to Glasgow and again in the cocktail bar at the airport hotel. I'm certain they had never met before.'

'Ah, weel,' he said, 'ye're entitled to your opinion. So ye believe Todd was leeing when he told Carbridge he had slept wi' her the night at the airport hotel?'

'Certainly I do! Besides, a man who would claim that, and, I suppose, boast about it, to a fellow like Carbridge is a skunk. There's not a word of truth in it, and I don't see Todd as that kind of a louse, anyway.'

'Oo, aye? Then wat about Rowardennan?'

I tried to think back. Rowardennan, on Loch Lomond, was where Hera and I had taken the trip across the water to Inverbeg. I remembered that Todd, with others of the youth hostellers not of our party, had crossed with us. He had given us a wave and a word, but, once ashore at Inverbeg, we had seen

no more of him. Hera and I, I remembered, had missed the
return boat and had spent the night at the hotel, crossing back
again in the morning. We had, as we had arranged, occupied
separate rooms at the hotel. There had been no sign of Todd on
the return trip and he was certainly with the others when they
set off next morning.

I said, 'Well, and what about Rowardennan? Todd didn't
spend the night at the hotel in Inverbeg. I would have known.'

'Ye *think* ye would have known, but let me tell ye, laddie,
wherever he spent the night, it was not in the Rowardennan
youth hostel. I would hae kenned that, better than ye would
hae kenned that he had your lassie tae bed.'

'Tell us more about the tour,' said Laura tactfully.

'I'll dae juist that,' said Perth, looking at her with gratitude.

I said, 'I'll take your word for it that he didn't spend the
night in the hostel with the rest of you. You *would* have known
about that, because of the dormitory system, but you will not
persuade me that he spent it at the hotel at Inverbeg. We would
have spotted him either there or when he got off the boat
coming back to Rowardennan the next morning.'

'Gang your ain gait,' said Perth. 'I willna press the point.'

I nodded, but my memory told me that at Crianlarich Todd
had suggested openly to Hera that he should escort her to the
hotel after the rumpus I had had with Carbridge. I began to
wonder, as the poison of suspicion lodged itself in my mind,
whether he would have made such a suggestion had he not had
some grounds for believing that she might fall in with it.

Dame Beatrice assisted in dissolving the tension somewhat
by asking whether anything had happened between Rowardennan and Crianlarich, while Hera and I were on our own and not
with the rest of the party.

I did not remember telling anybody in particular that just
before Hera and I reached the hostel at Crianlarich we had come
upon Perth and the students busy with their hammers and
chisels and all the rest of their geological gear, but I suppose
I must have done, or she would not have followed up her
question by remarking that it was on that part of The Way that

there appeared to have been some slight evidence of dissension.

According to Perth, the trouble, if that is not too strong and misleading a word, began on the stretch between Rowardennan and Inversnaid. There was a rather pointless argument between Tansy and Carbridge about the name of a spectacular mountain — Carbridge claiming that it was called the Cobbler, Tansy maintaining that it was Ben Arthur.

'But both are right,' Laura interposed at this point. 'Ben Arthur *is* the Cobbler. There are three peaks and these, seen against the skyline, are supposed to represent a cobbler, his wife and his daughter, or some such rubbish. As a matter of fact, the Cobbler is only the anglicised way of pronouncing the Gaelic An Gobaileach, the *g* being spoken like a *k* or a hard *c*. The Gaelic name has nothing to do with shoe-mending. It simply means 'forked peak'. The 'Arthur' I imagine is the name given it for territorial reasons by a clan or sept. The MacArthurs, in a sense, are Campbells, but they claim seniority. When Ewan Campbell resigned his lands in the fourteenth century, King Robert the Second granted them to Arthur Campbell, the son, wherefore the peak was named Arthur, I suppose as a claim to it.'

We all listened to this with the uneasy respect which is accorded to a knowledgeable purveyor of useless information. Laura sensed immediately that the audience was becoming restive. She waved a shapely hand in apology and said, 'Sorry. I get carried away. Anyhow, what a stupid thing for those two to argue about.'

'Yes, it hardly seems a matter of life and death,' said Dame Beatrice, bringing us back to the real seriousness of the matter in hand. 'What happened after that?'

It appeared that Rhoda had taken up the subject in support of her friend and then had said that the pace set by Todd and Carbridge was turning what ought to be a pleasant ramble into a marathon race. Jane Minch had joined in to complain that her feet were hurting her, but her brother had pointed out that going more slowly was not the best remedy. Better, he said, to push on and get a longer rest at the end of the day.

'What of the students?' asked Dame Beatrice. 'I understand from Mr Melrose that they too preferred to linger a little on The Way.' (That, of course, although again I did not remember telling anybody about it, had begun at Inchcailloch, the Loch Lomond island which Hera and I had not visited. It was to do with the geological survey.) However, it did not seem that there had been any more serious disputes among the party. The men, in fact, had taken it in turns to carry Jane's rucksack as well as their own, the exception being Trickett, who said that, with the extra equipment the geologists carried, he was physically incapable of knight-errantry.

'Did you yourself lend a hand to beauty in distress?' said Dame Beatrice to Perth.

'Oo aye, I did my share, but the going, in some places, was verra severe on a lassie wi' sair feet, even if she wasna hampered wi' her gear.'

'Would you say that any one person in the party took a particular dislike to Carbridge?' asked Dame Beatrice. Perth shook his head and answered that the nearest to that would be the two clerks, Tansy and Rhoda. For one thing, he said, Tansy in particular had an eye on Todd and found Carbridge, with his extreme mateyness and his determination to keep his flock together and permit no straying for purposes of dalliance, extremely frustrating and irritating.

'Although I'm bound to tell ye,' said Perth, 'that the man Todd showed nae disposition to respond to her female wiles. Gin his een strayed ony place when Miss Camden wisna wi' us, it would hae been that he lookit at the student Patsy Carlow.'

I said nothing, but I could have remarked that, if Todd's thoughts were on Hera, he would hardly have looked twice at Tansy, anyway. Although, as I had thought when first I met her and Rhoda, Tansy was probably kind-hearted, she could scarcely be called glamorous. The forthcoming and much younger Patsy might be a different proposition.

'The twa clerks left the party at Crianlarich,' Perth went on. 'They didna spend the night at the hostel, but went on to Fort William and there we met them again. Myself and the students spent three days in the hills and slept at the Crianlarich youth hostel, while the ither four — Todd, Carbridge and the Minches, went on. We were a wee thing hindered by mist, but guid work was done to the satisfaction o' the students and we also took transport, as did the women Parks and Green, to get ourselves to Fort William.'

'Did you do anything there apart from climbing the mountain?' asked Laura.

'Oo, aye. There are shops in the toon, ye'll ken, and lassies always go wild when there are shops. Souvenirs were purchased and displayed, for, as we were all intending to take the train when we had put in three nights at the youth hostel at Fort William, there was little need to fash about a little extra weight in the packs and the students could leave everything at the hostel while we climbed the mountain.'

'What kind of things did they buy?' asked Laura.

'Och, what you would expect. Rhoda had a tweed for a skirt, Patsy bought Todd a wee present of a knife and Tansy, also fu' of improper thoughts about Todd, I'm thinking, purchased, at an awfu' lang price — but, of course, she earned money in her job — she bought him a knife, too. It was a genuine antique. Patsy's knife was an imitation of a *sgian dubh*.'

'A *sgian dubh*, eh?' said Laura.

'Ye'll be thinking on the murder,' said Perth, 'but gin ye think yon man Todd would stab a fellow creature in the back, as I am telled was done tae Carbridge, ye hae Todd summed up wrangly, Mistress Gavin.'

'The stabbing, as I understand it, was only a *coup de grâce* in case the strangling hadn't done the job completely,' I reminded the company.

'Oo, aye, verra like,' agreed Perth. 'I hae to tell ye, mistress,' he added, addressing Laura again, 'as I hae been speired at tae mention purchases, that Jane Minch made purchase of some beautiful notepaper wi' headings o' the Loch Ness monster and various flowers and birds and knights on horseback — verra fine indeed.'

'From the Malin Workshop in Claggan Road,' I said. 'Hera

bought some, too. Beautiful drawings. Hedderwick, I remember, is the artist's name. Did anybody else purchase anything in the nature of a weapon?'

'The maist o' them made a purchase,' said Perth, 'but naebody else bought a knife. There was the fake *sgian dubh* and the knife bought by the woman Tansy Parks. She had it frae a shop which sold antiques. I was wi' her when she bought it and I wrestled vairbally wi' the proprietor on her behalf tae hae the price reduced. "Ye'll ne'er get your money for that bauble," I was telling him. "A' the visitors are requiring are souvenirs. Not by ony length is that knife a souvenir o' a trip to Fort William. It's no even o' Scottish manufacture." '

'So what sort of dagger was it?' asked Laura.

'I am not convairsant wi' the history o' dirks, but, according tae the man, it was Spanish-made in about 1878, and to my mind there was naething so verra special aboot it. It was not what I would ca' an object o' distinction, but the lassie fancied it. It was broadish and the blade would ha' been, in my reckoning, aboot seven inches in length and the knife overall aboot fifteen inches, but there wasna a sheath wi' it. He had anither, a verra superior specimen, wi' a tortoiseshell and mother o' pearl handle, but the price was quite inordinate, so she took the first ane.'

'What made her choose such an object?' asked Dame Beatrice.

'She said she wanted to mak' a gift of it, but she didna then say to whom. As I telled ye, my thought upon it was that she intended to gift it to Todd.'

'What you tell us is of the greatest interest,' said Dame Beatrice. 'Do the police know about all this?'

'I dinna ken.'

We learned later what had happened to Patsy's knife. Chagrined to find her gift redundant when she discovered the destination of Tansy's purchase, she had raffled it when the students got back and it had been won by Freddie Brown.

## 15
## *Talking Things Over*

The warden had the address of the women students' hall of residence and Dame Beatrice obtained it from him before she left. He would be glad, he said, to have the mystery of Carbridge's death cleared up before the new term began, if that were possible. He added that the police were making heavy weather of their investigations and that it was very hard on those students who had done such good work in Scotland during their summer vacation that they should be under harassment when they were all completely innocent.

Privately, I think, Dame Beatrice was keeping an open mind about their guilt or innocence, but she could hardly tell this to anybody in the warden's position. I walked round to Hera's flat when the goodnights had been said and found her, as I had expected, awaiting me and alone. Whether Todd had been quite as good as his word I did not know, but, at any rate, he was not in her flat when I arrived.

'Well,' she said, 'how did things go? Did Dame Beatrice extort a confession of guilt from anybody?'

'As you would expect, some useful information emerged. Perth was particularly enlightening.'

'That man has eyes and ears everywhere. I suppose both were necessary in the job he had to do on the tour. It can't have been easy with that little horror Patsy Carlow in the party.'

'He made two interesting disclosures which may or may not have some bearing on Carbridge's death and he also let a few other cats out of bags which, so far as I can see, have nothing to do with murder, but which highlight what I may call the love interest.'

'Oh, Lord!'

'Yes, indeed.'

'Well, out with it, if you've come here to make a scene.'

'Why should I do that?'

'Oh, that's all right, then. What happened? What was said?'

'It's getting late. Let's leave it until tomorrow. It may turn out to be a long story.'

So we arranged that I should take her out to dinner the next evening and then that we should return to her flat for our talk. When the appointed time arrived, she came straight to the point which concerned the two of us most closely.

'I suppose Perth told you about Todd and me,' she said.

It staggered me that she should refer to Todd so openly and in so calm a manner. I was nonplussed by her frankness and said feebly, 'Well, yes, sort of, yes, he did.'

'The snooping old cub-leader! What did he tell you?'

'That Todd slept at the Inverbeg hotel on the same night as we did.'

'Yes, he did. He pushed on ahead of the others and, although you didn't see him, he crossed on the ferry when we did, but if Perth told you I slept with him, it's not true.'

'No?'

'No. I didn't mean for this to come out just yet, Comrie, but I would have told you all about it later, when things were settled.'

'What about Glasgow?'

'Perth couldn't have told you about Glasgow. He knew nothing about what happened at the airport hotel. Oh, dear! I wish he hadn't taken the bull by the horns, the wretched man! Anyway, he did, so I must make the best of it. You had the impression, when I met Todd on the train and again at the airport hotel, that he was a stranger to me. I tried to give you a hint that this was not the case, but you were too thick to catch on.'

'Oh, was I? But I have a trusting nature, you see.'

'Don't you remember that crack of mine about people with two left feet?'

'Vividly. I have seldom felt more embarrassed.'

'You surely didn't think I would say a thing like that to somebody I had only just met?'

'It seemed out of character, I admit, but I thought you were annoyed by his attempting to pick you up.'

'You always have been a myopic old soul where I am concerned. Don't you remember my calling him *Sweeney* Todd later? That would have been another frightful liberty if we hadn't known one another very well. Anyway, thanks to that idiotic Carbridge and your own fixations, Glasgow and Inverbeg were the only chances Barney and I had to get together and talk over our plans for a divorce.'

'*What!*'

'Yes. I married him when I was — well, a whole lot younger than I am now. It didn't work out very well, and we separated, but nothing legal was involved. It wasn't even a judicial separation. We agreed to go our separate ways and then, when the legal period of irreparable breakdown of the marriage was over, to arrange for a divorce.'

'What didn't you like about him?'

'He was a male chauvinist pig,' she said lightly.

'Expound, as Dame Beatrice would say.' (Strange to say, the shock her disclosure had given me was already dying away.)

'You know,' said Hera, 'you're taking this very calmly. I thought you would rant and roar.'

'That is only done by true British sailors and even then, according to the song, they need to be on the high seas.' To be truthful, my calmness in the face of her confession surprised nobody more than myself. I touched the pocket in which I still had her engagement ring. The little circlet seemed to have turned into some sort of talisman. I found comfort in the realisation that it was in my possession and not on her finger.

'Well, I'm not flattered,' she said, 'by the way you've taken news which I thought would stun you. Anyway, you asked what I didn't like about Barney. Looking back, I don't really know. He was tall, handsome, free with his money, a most satisfactory escort and I suppose that, in a way, I liked him very much. The trouble was that I wanted a career for myself and it was because of my insistence on this that we fell out. After our honeymoon I refused to sleep with him until he gave up trying to turn me into a good wife and mother, so he picked up a girl and we parted.'

'And I got you on the rebound.'

'Heavens, no! You mustn't think that, Comrie. I'm very fond of you and had you taken me into partnership — '

'That business on the train,' I said, cutting in before she could get into her stride. 'Was it pre-arranged?'

'No, it wasn't, but the meeting at the airport hotel was. Todd had had no intention of walking The Way until I told him in the train corridor of our plans, yours and mine, to test ourselves and find out how well we could get along with one another under primitive conditions.'

'Oh, come now! When we met him again at the Glasgow youth hostel, he was all equipped for a walking tour. He must have had it planned.'

'Plenty of shops in Glasgow where he could have bought the gear he needed and he had all the time in the world to equip himself while you were dragging me around the main features of the city.'

I stuck to my guns and said, 'You can't just walk into a youth hostel and ask for accommodation.'

'He had had a hosteller's card for years. He wasn't always as prosperous as he was when he married me.'

'Suppose the hostel had been full?'

'Well, it wasn't, was it?' she said impatiently. 'I expect that, after he had shown up at the airport hotel and got his key, he went straight out again to wedge himself in at the hostel for the following night so as to coincide with our arrival there. Do you remember that I would not stay a second night at the hotel?'

'So you slept with him at the airport hotel on the only night we were all three there!'

'I did nothing of the kind, or at Inverbeg, either. Believe what you please, but that is the truth. I went to his room, not he to mine, and we had a business conversation, that's all.'

'Did you, so to speak, get anything fixed up about a divorce?'
I asked sardonically.

She replied in all seriousness, 'Not at the time. Now tell me
about Perth and the discussion in the warden's lodgings.'

'Why didn't you tell me you were married to Todd?'

'Do you want the truth or a nice coat of veneer?'

'Come on! Out with it, please. I've a right to know.'

'Oh, you men and your rights! I didn't tell you at first because I wanted to marry you and I thought it might not come
off if you knew too soon that I had to get a divorce before I
could take you on a permanent basis, and I had no intention of
getting run in for committing bigamy, I assure you. I have never
lost touch with Barney, but meeting him like that on the train
to Glasgow was entirely a surprise.'

'Would you be mortally offended if I said I do not believe
you?'

'No, I shouldn't be offended, but you must admit that coin-
cidences do occur. You, of all people, have to accept that they
do. What about your two dead bodies?'

'I've thought a lot about them, naturally, and I don't believe there was coincidence. I have come to the conclusion that
the death of Carbridge was a copy-cat murder.'

'How do you mean?'

'Ask yourself. Strangulation is a method of murdering
people. Right?'

'Certainly.'

'Stabbing people in the back is another but a very dissimilar
method.'

'Agreed and I suppose I see what you mean.'

'Yes. When the two methods are used on a second body
within a matter of weeks, one tends to suppose either that the
same murderer has repeated his method or that somebody else
has copied it.'

'You haven't really proved your point, but I agree with you
that it does provide food for thought. Would you have broken
our engagement if you had known earlier about Barney and
me?'

'If I had known you were waiting for a divorce before I could marry you, I doubt whether we should ever have been engaged to one another at all.'

'Well, that's straight from the shoulder, anyway. *Now* will you tell me about Dame Beatrice and what you were told at the warden's lodgings?'

I was at last prepared to change the subject.

'Perth was our chief spokesman,' I said. 'That is why he was invited to the dinner, of course. He voiced the opinion that Carbridge was a fool.'

'Well, that wasn't a very original thought. Everybody knew Carbridge was a fool and a tiresomely boring fool at that. Even Tansy and Rhoda thought so.'

'Perth gave me the impression that Carbridge was killed *because* he was a fool.'

'I suppose there have been less valid reasons for killing people. One aspect of Carbridge's foolishness was that one couldn't trust him not to babble, but I suppose the same could be said of young James Minch. What else was there?'

'Oh, that people bought souvenirs in Fort William.'

'People do buy souvenirs when they're on holiday, so there's nothing surprising in that.'

'Two of the souvenirs appear to have been of a lethal nature. They were daggers. One was bought by Tansy and the other by Patsy.'

'Has anybody told that to Bingley?'

'I have no idea. The trouble is that the people who bought them didn't keep them. As far as we know, one was given to Todd and young Freddie Brown won the other in a raffle. It, too, was meant as a gift to Todd, but Patsy changed her mind when she heard about Tansy's present. I don't suppose Todd wanted to accept a gift from either of the women.'

'Thank goodness for that! I shouldn't like to think I was married to a murderer.'

I ignored what I thought was a flippant remark.

'Is our engagement off for good?' I asked.

'You made that very clear a short while ago, didn't you?'

'It was you who broke things up in the first place.'

'Oh, my dear Comrie, I've been doubtful about us for a long time. The tour only crystallised my ideas.'

'We got on all right on the tour.'

'When you were rabbit enough to accept my rulings? No intimacy for a fortnight? I want a man, not a mouse.'

'Well, I'm damned!'

'Yes, with faint praise for behaving like a gentleman when what I wanted was to see the wolf emerge from the sheep's clothing. Do you remember the gypsy at Inverarnan?'

'You wouldn't tell me what she said.'

'I couldn't, at the time, because I had not finally made up my mind about you, but I can tell you now. She said that the man I was with was not the man for me. She was right, Comrie. I have no use for a man I can dominate.'

'You might have seen a different side of me when we were married. You did not get your own way about joining my firm.'

'Oh, that was Sandy, not you. I could have overruled you easily enough if there had been nobody else to contend with. Anyway, neither of you need have insulted me by taking that woman Elsa Moore into partnership.'

'Let's not argue about that. To make Elsa a partner was a necessity if we wanted to keep her.'

'Only marriage to one of you would make absolutely sure of that.'

'It's up to Sandy, then,' I said laughingly.

'Are you going to tell Bingley about the souvenir daggers?'

'Not I. It is none of my business. Dame Beatrice was present and I'm sure she'll take the necessary steps.'

When I got back to my flat, I took out what had been the engagement ring, reflected somewhat ruefully on what I had had to pay for it, packed it up very carefully and wrote a covering note.

'Please do me the honour of keeping our ring. I don't want any other woman to wear it. It will fit your right hand as a dress ring and Todd won't worry that I gave it to you. I have the feeling that, as soon as this dreadful business about poor

Carbridge is cleared up, you will go back to your Barney. Anyway, the very best of luck to you both.' I ended with a quotation from John Donne which seemed appropriate under the circumstances:

> 'Now thou hast lov'd me one whole day,
> Tomorrow when thou leav'st, what wilt thou say?
> Wilt thou then ante-date some new-made vow?
> Or say that now
> We are not just those persons which we were?'

'You seem remarkably bobbish,' said Elsa when I got to the office next day. 'Have we had a rebate from the taxman?'

'Not from the taxman,' I said, 'but I suppose I've had a wind-fall of a sort.'

'Are we to be treated to champagne?'

'No, only to the funeral bakemeats.'

She looked at me with mock concern and said that she was very sorry to hear it, but she asked no questions and the office routine went on much as usual until lunchtime. Sandy asked Elsa to join us at our favourite pub, for we took only a snack and a beer at midday. She refused and he said to me when we had obtained refreshment and were seated at our little table, 'What's eating Elsa? When I asked her to join us, she said, "Three's a crowd and Comrie has something to tell you." Have you something to tell me?'

'I could tell you that Perth knows of two daggers which were bought as souvenirs in Fort William. I think Dame Beatrice will hand this bit of information to the police and leave Bingley to sort it out. The two women who bought the daggers intended to give them as presents to Todd. The point of interest now is to discover who did what with them when the tour was over.'

'You would need to know whether one of them was the weapon which somebody stuck in Carbridge's back, wouldn't you? That weapon, according to the papers, has never been found, has it?'

'No. There was an ordinary kitchen knife in the body, but

the forensic chaps know it was planted after the death wound
was dealt and the murder weapon pulled out.'

'Yes. Elsa wasn't talking about the murder when she said that
three is a crowd. Come clean, Comrie. She was hinting at something.'

'Elsa is too clever by half when it comes to reading people's
minds.'

'Granted. That's why she is so valuable to us, so now out
with it. What has happened to make her think you are so light-
hearted that you prevent yourself only with the greatest difficulty from going about the office with a song on your lips? Has
Hera thought better of it and asked for the ring again?'

'Quite the opposite. We have agreed to part company for
ever and ever, *amen*.'

'Thank goodness for that! Now I can tell you something
which I've been bottling up ever since I came back from my
holiday.'

'Sweden? I should hardly have thought of that as a holiday.
Did you strike lucky with a sort of young Greta Garbo?'

'Don't hedge! You know the holiday I'm talking about.'

'You got mugged, you ass. At least I avoided *that* when I was
on The Way.'

'Yes, I got mugged. Did it never strike you as strange that I
made no attempt to go to the police?'

'No, it didn't strike me as strange at all. Neither did *I* go to
the police when I found that body in those ruins on Rannoch
Moor.'

'Our motives were very different, Comrie.'

'I shouldn't think so. Scottish law is what is different. Like
me, you did not want to get mixed up with it. We are busy men
and to bring in the Scottish police would have meant sacri-
ficing a lot of valuable time and, ten to one, they wouldn't
have tracked down your assailant.'

'Oh, I would sacrifice any amount of time to bring even one
mugger, let alone a rapist, to book,' said Sandy. 'It would be a
public duty and I should not shirk it. No, it was not that. You
see, I had a pretty good idea of the identity of my attacker.'

'Some frenzied author whose book we have been unable to place?' (I was playing for time, although I knew that this was only a question of procrastination. I should have to hear his unwelcome views in the end. I felt that already I knew what they were going to be.)

'I can give you a name, but not that of a disgruntled author. The person who attempted to lay me out — no, perhaps, after all, I had better not say.'

'You mean you think it was Hera. That is impossible. She was modelling in Paris all that week,' I said.

'But she wasn't, Comrie. I found that out before I ever went up to Scotland.'

'You old fox! Whatever made you do that?' I felt I ought to be angry with him, but it would have been nothing more than a gesture. Hera meant nothing to me any more. There was no need for me to defend her.

'Elsa put me up to it in a way. She asked me whether you and I realised how angry Hera was when we refused to take her into partnership. I said I had a pretty good idea and that I knew how much Hera hated being thwarted. Elsa said, "Sandy, she will stop at nothing. If you were not behind him, Comrie would give in to her. Do look out for yourself." Well, you know Elsa. She never takes panic stations, so I thought it might be just as well to find out what Hera was planning while I was safely out of the way.'

'You surely didn't think I would agree in your absence to anything which so closely affected us both?'

'No, of course I didn't think that, but, well — '

We finished our snack of a meal in silence. I knew there was more that he could tell me, but the pub was closing for the afternoon and in any case I wanted time to think. As I had received the news of Hera's marriage to Todd, so I received this fresh view of her conduct. That is to say, I was so far from being shattered by it that all I remember feeling was intense curiosity concerning the activities of a woman I had imagined I knew well.

I even found myself trying to work out, with cold logic and

in an entirely unemotional way, whether it was she who had killed Carbridge. At any rate, my cogitations reached a satisfactory conclusion on that point. If the medical evidence concerning time of death was correct even within a couple of hours — and the doctors themselves, I thought, had given rigor mortis ample scope — there was no way on earth that Hera could have had the opportunity to put a knife in the man's back on that Saturday afternoon. As for strangling him beforehand, she had neither the physical strength nor the complete lack of squeamishness to attempt such a method of inducing death. Neither did I believe that, had she indeed been the mugger, she would have intended any more harm to Sandy than to put him out of action for a week or so.

At half-past three Elsa herself came into my office with two cups of tea, her own and mine.

'What?' I said. 'The queen of Sheba waiting upon King Solomon? Has the typing pool Hebe gone on strike?'

She set down the cups and took a seat.

'I have just dismissed Luella Granville Waterman from these sacrosanct precincts,' she said. 'I was sure you had forgotten that she had an appointment with you at a quarter to three, so I didn't send her in.'

We had a habit of referring to our more difficult and obstreperous authors by names culled from *Psmith, Journalist*. This helped to keep us sane and good-humoured in dealing with them, and again was Elsa's idea.

'Good Lord!' I said. 'I had forgotten all about her!'

'A fact which, in your interests, I failed to mention to her.'

'Did you contrive to soothe that savage breast?'

'What else do you pay me for? I'm to let her know tomorrow the doctor's report. I said he was still with you.'

'What on earth are you talking about?'

'You hover between life and death, dear. It was only by convincing her of that hardly self-evident fact that I could persuade her to leave. But that is not the reason for my being here and ministering unto you with my own delicate hands.'

'Any excuse for a session with you is as good as any other.

So to what am I indebted?' I asked.

'Do you know what unpardonable liberties are?'

'I ought to.'

'Oh, you mean when you punched a man in the eye for attempting to put his arm round Hera. I heard about that. Well, I am about to tell you of an unpardonable liberty I took because, if I don't confess it, Sandy will tell you that it was he who took it.'

'He has told me already, I think. He checked on Hera's visit to Paris.'

'As a matter of fact, *I* did. She did not go to Paris. I know which agents she uses for her modelling jobs and it seemed to me very strange that she should be going off to Paris just when Sandy was going to be out of London and you and I were to be left holding the fort here.'

'So she didn't go to Paris. She went to Scotland and did her damnedest to disable Sandy. I find that difficult to believe, you know.'

'Suit yourself.' She drank her tea. I pushed my cup aside.

'It's utterly ridiculous,' I said, 'and neither of you has any proof at all.'

'With Sandy out of the way, she could have worked on you to take her into the partnership.'

'What about you? Wouldn't you have had something to say?'

'I wasn't a partner at that time. I should have chucked my job, of course. I could never work with Hera.'

'Anyway,' I said, 'strong-arm stuff is not her line. Whoever clocked Sandy in those woods or wherever it was made a boss shot. That's the only reason I'm prepared to admit it *could* have been Hera. I still don't believe it was.'

'Typical of a woman who was not used to what you call strong-arm stuff. A real mugger would have made a much better job of it.'

'What did Luella Granville Waterman want to see me about?' (I was anxious to change the subject.)

'That's right. When defeated in argument, always take a different line. What *she* wants to change is her publisher.'

'But because old Timothy once had an affair with her mother, Timothy's sons have been publishing that bilge of hers for years.'

'They haven't lost on it, you know. She's got her following.'

'Heaven help them! What do I say to her tomorrow?'

'She isn't coming tomorrow. I have promised to let her know when you are out of danger. I have also told her we'll try Peregrines if she likes, but that they start new authors at only seven and a half on the first five thousand. That ought to shake her. Oh, and by the way, I'm going to marry Sandy.'

'Not me?' I spoke jokingly, but the news took me completely by surprise.

'No, dear, not you. My union doesn't allow me to accept other women's leavings,' she said, getting up from her chair.

'You devil!' I said. I caught her and kissed her. 'I hope you will be very, very happy. Good old Sandy! I had no idea!'

'Well, you don't have many ideas, do you, dear?' she said. 'You should have got a line on your Hera months ago.'

# 16

## The Rounding-Up

So, all these extraneous details being settled, we were back to the murder. Hera was a late riser when she was not working, so at nine the next morning I went to her flat and pushed through her letter-box the package containing the ring. This meant that I arrived at the office earlier than usual, for Sandy and I did not show up usually until ten.

I found Elsa busy dealing with the morning's correspondence.

'My, my!' she said. 'Couldn't we sleep? Was our conscience troubling us? That policeman has been here asking to see you. I told him to try again later.'

'What does he want, I wonder? There is nothing I can tell him about myself that he doesn't know already.'

A telephone call came through half an hour later. Polly answered it and put Bingley through to me. I said I would be charmed to see him whenever he wanted an interview and he replied to this that he would come round at once. Sandy had arrived before Bingley turned up, so, when I had congratulated him on his engagement to Elsa, I told him what was in the wind and prophesied (rightly, as it happened) that somebody under pressure had magnified the story of my punch-up with Carbridge at Crianlarich.

I took Bingley into my office, told Elsa to see that we were not disturbed and waited for Bingley's opening gambit. It was what I had expected.

'You had a serious disagreement with the deceased while you were on your Scottish tour, Mr Melrose.'

'Disagreement, yes. Serious, no.'

'It concerned your fiancée, Miss Camden.'

'May I point out that you are behind the times, Detective Chief Inspector? Not my fiancée any longer, and not Miss Camden. Try Mrs Todd.'

'Are you serious, sir?'

'Oh, yes. The walking tour was an experiment before Mrs Todd applied for a divorce so that she could marry me. The result has told us both where we stand — apart.'

'What you tell me lends a different aspect to the matters arising. The reports I have received may have been somewhat exaggerated, sir.'

'A bit of luck for me, if you think so.'

'Yes, you may say that, sir. I shall need to check this new piece of information before taking further steps. Mrs *Todd*, you say?'

'Alas, yes. Love's young dream is over, so far as I am concerned.'

He looked at me and at the flower in my buttonhole. It was a pink rosebud given me by Polly because, she said, it looked festive and so did I. Bingley must have agreed with her, for he said that I appeared to be taking my bereavement extremely well. He left soon after he had said that, and I had the impression that he was a baffled man. I wondered whether he had come to the office with a warrant for my arrest. Of one thing I was certain. If he had received an exaggerated account of the punch-up, it would have come from one of three people. It could have been from Hera herself, from Todd (with whom I had exchanged words, although not blows) or Perth. There was a possible fourth, namely James Minch, always ready with a rush of words to the mouth. Neither he nor Perth would have intended any harm, but they might have done my cause a great deal of mischief, all the same.

Whichever one of them it was, there could be no doubt that I had given Bingley something to think about and, as any respite is to be preferred to sudden death, I was grateful for it. I expected Bingley to return later in the day, but he did not do so and the next step in the solution to his problem came in the form of a telephone call to me from Dame Beatrice. She had been called upon officially in her capacity as psychiatric adviser to the Home Office, she said, and at Bingley's request.

'I have to question certain members of the Scottish expedition,' she said. 'I shall take Laura with me to record the interviews, but I need your support in reassuring my suspects.'

'Perth would be far more useful.'

'Laura said that you would jib.'

'No, no, I'm not jibbing. Of course I'll do anything you say.'

'The police,' said Dame Beatrice in a reminiscent tone, 'are seldom wrong when they have very definite suspicions that they know the identity of a criminal, but sometimes there are factors which they do not take into account.'

'You mean Bingley thinks he knows who murdered Carbridge?'

'Yes, and I can follow his reasoning, although I do not think he is right.'

'But you have to find proof?' I said.

She cackled. 'Yes, indeed. I have to find proof, and when I find it he may be somewhat surprised.'

'So you think he has set his sights on the wrong person?'

'There are factors he has not taken into account.'

'For instance?' I looked for enlightenment, but it did not come. All that she added was: 'Cast your mind back to the one evening you and Miss Camden spent at Fort William. Can you remember whether the home addresses of the various parties were exchanged? I know that Mr Trickett had a list, or he could not have sent out the invitations, but I think there must have been others.'

'Oh, yes, there was a good deal of writing down and promising to keep in touch and all that kind of thing, but, anyway, I suppose people could have found out during the tour where other people lived if they were interested enough. Trickett, as you say, must have had a complete list. I believe he was the only person who asked for Hera's address and mine. We were rather the odd men out because we had been with the rest of them so little.'

'Then I think a telephone call to Mr Trickett will be sufficient for my purpose. Perhaps you would be good enough to make it for me. Ask whether Miss Coral Platt or Mr Freddie Brown is a home student. They were the two in charge of the catering at the students' party, I am told.'

'Ah!' I said. 'The kitchen knife that was found in the body and which was not the knife the pathologist thinks was the murder weapon.'

So, my having ascertained from Trickett that Coral was a home student but that Freddie was a boarder at the hall of residence during term-time, Dame Beatrice herself did the telephoning and fixed up an appointment with Coral for the following evening. Coral's father insisted on being present at the interview and to this Dame Beatrice made no objection. She came straight to the point.

'Where did you get the vegetable knife?' she asked.

Coral looked distressed. I think she might have refused to answer the question, but her father said, 'Speak up. Let's have done with all this moping and worry. Your mother and I knew something was wrong. We thought you were pining over a love affair, but it sounds more serious than that. I'm sure Dame Beatrice knows you had nothing to do with that shocking affair.' He put his hand over the girl's and she turned her palm and clasped his fingers. Then she spoke out resolutely.

'I borrowed the vegetable knife from our kitchen,' she said. 'I knew we were going to have hamburgers at the party, so I thought it would come in useful for chopping up the onions. I like a knife I'm used to and I didn't know what sort of cutlery I should find at the men's hall.'

'I am afraid you will have to identify the knife which the police have in their possession,' said Dame Beatrice, 'but do not be afraid. We know the murder was not committed with it. It was used merely as a substitute. The inference is that, if the lethal weapon had been found, it would have given a clue to the identity of the killer.'

'I wonder why he left Coral's knife in the body and did not get rid of that, as well as his own weapon?' I said.

'He reasoned, no doubt, that Miss Platt's knife would not be traced to him. Now, Miss Platt, you borrowed the vegetable knife from your mother's kitchen. When did you realise that it had disappeared from the hall of residence?'

'When Freddie and I got back from tea. We went to a Wimpy's and when we got back the knife was gone, but I didn't worry too much at the time because I had chopped up the onions — more, actually, than I thought we should need — before we went out to tea. It was after — well, you know — after we knew that a kitchen knife had been found in the body — '

'Yes,' said Dame Beatrice, 'do not distress yourself. When you knew that, you connected it with the disappearance of your own knife. Did the caretaker Bull come into the kitchen while you and Mr Freddie Brown were making your preparations?'

'No, I'm sure he didn't. He was helping in various ways, but I don't remember him in the kitchen.'

'When the police ask you to identify the knife, have no fear. As it was not the murder weapon, it has only secondary interest for them.'

Then we visited Freddie Brown. He was at the hall of residence and was cutting sections of rock plants and looking at them under a microscope. Sunny-tempered as ever, he showed no sign of resentment at being interrupted.

'Now, Mr Brown,' said Dame Beatrice, 'you may remember that, when preparations were being made for the students' party, a small knife with which Miss Platt had been chopping onions was missing.'

'Yes. We didn't worry much, at least, not at the time. We thought one of the others had come into the kitchen and whipped it for some reason. There were quite a lot of people milling about, helping to get things ready. It was only when I read about the knife found in the body and told Coral that she began to panic. She begged me to say nothing to anybody about her loss of the knife, so, of course, I promised. Anyway, we don't know that the knife *was* her knife, do we?'

'We shall know when she identifies it,' said Dame Beatrice.

'Oh, I say! You're not going to make the poor girl do that, are you? They don't think it was that little knife which did the damage, but I suppose nobody but the murderer would have left it in the body.'

'Quite so. Now, Mr Brown, to another matter: will you tell me whether you remember purchasing a souvenir in Fort William?'

'Not me; hadn't got the cash and didn't see anything I wanted except a Caithness decanter which I couldn't possibly afford. Some people bought things, but not me.'

'Some people bought daggers, for example.'

'Yes, two of the women who were hoping that Todd would — well — '

'Extend his favours to them?'

'I suppose you could put it like that, but, as Coral said to me, anybody could see with half an eye that they didn't stand an earthly. He had his sights on — ' He looked at me and left the sentence unfinished.

'Yes, I understand that Mr Todd refused to accept the gifts and that subsequently they passed into other hands,' said Dame Beatrice.

'Well, if you want to know, one of them passed into *my* hands,' said Freddie. 'I don't know what happened to the other, but I got one in a raffle.'

'Ah, yes, the weapon which was more than a hundred years old and therefore passed as an antique.'

'Oh, no, absolutely not that beastly thing! I expect Todd kept that. It was valuable. The one that got raffled was the *sgian dubh*. I had just enough money to take a ticket and it seemed a suitable souvenir, being of the Highlands and all that. Minch laughed when the girl showed it off to the others before she tried to give it to Todd. Minch said it was only a toy and that he had a real one which he would show her sometime. I've got mine in my room. Would you like to see it?'

'Very much,' said Dame Beatrice. He was not gone long. He came back with the little dagger. It had a silver-mounted black sheath with a whacking great cairngorm stuck in the handle. Dame Beatrice looked it over and handed it to Laura. Their eyes met and I saw Laura shake her head. She remarked that some girls had more money than sense.

'Well, thank you, Mr Brown,' said Dame Beatrice. Laura handed back the *sgian dubh* and, as we were leaving, Freddie said nervously that he hoped he had not welshed on anybody. It had been a good tour and he had been glad he went on it until all this rotten business had followed on.

When I got back to my flat that night a most uneasy idea came into my mind. I mean, by that, an idea which made *me* uneasy. When Dame Beatrice and Laura came next day to my office and told me that they had an afternoon appointment with the Minches and hoped I would accompany them, I came out promptly and explosively with what was on my mind.

'Look here,' I said, addressing Laura instead of challenging Dame Beatrice's brilliant black eyes, 'you are not doing a Roger Ackroyd on me, are you?'

'The elliptical form of your question nevertheless makes your meaning clear,' said Dame Beatrice. 'No, my dear Comrie, we have no Hercule Poirot up our sleeves. Your presence is merely to assure our patients (if I may call them so) of the respectability and open-mindedness of our intentions. Do you forget that you also have been a patient of mine?'

'Meaning that she knows you from soup to nuts, to borrow a phrase from my favourite author,' said Laura. 'So be not afraid, neither be thou dismayed (to borrow from yet another source of inspiration), so buck up. All is not lost.'

'What was wrong with Freddie's *sgian dubh*?' I asked.

Dame Beatrice nodded to Laura, who replied, 'Nothing was *wrong* with it, but those silver mountings were hardly hall-marked and the blade, when I examined it, was hardly a thing of tempered steel. In other words, I would take my oath that, wherever Freddie Brown's *sgian dubh* came from, it is merely the tourist catchpenny implement James Minch despised and thereupon, if I am not mistaken, hangs a very interesting tale,' said Laura.

'And that is why we are going to visit the Minch family,' said Dame Beatrice. 'I am now working in close collaboration with Detective Chief Inspector Bingley and he tells me that James

Minch denied having a *sgian dubh* in his stocking at the students' party, though he admitted he had one at home.'

The Minches lived with their parents in a very pleasant house amid Oxshott woodlands. A maid answered the door. Dame Beatrice sent in her card and Jane Minch came along. Her father and James, she said, were playing golf and her mother had gone to a matinée. She asked us in and seated us.

'I thought we were to meet your brother,' said Dame Beatrice mildly.

'My father says James talks too much, and he does, of course,' said Jane. 'My father says that anything James could tell you I can tell you equally well, and that is true, too.'

'I am sure it is. What happened to the *sgian dubh* which your brother was questioned about after the murder?'

'James wanted to get rid of it when that policeman seemed so interested in it, so he tried to sell it.'

'I gather that he was unsuccessful,' said Dame Beatrice.

'Yes, he was, so we've still got the thing. It's in his room. Do you want to see it?' She went upstairs and came down with it. It was a lovely little thing, silver-mounted in a black sheath, elegant and slim, a replica, in fact, of the one Freddie Brown had shown us, but the genuine article, not a fake.

'If he wants to sell that,' said Laura, 'and the price is fair, I'm in the market.'

'Why did he become alarmed when the police interested themselves in this very charming little knife?' asked Dame Beatrice. Jane came over to me and seated herself on the arm of my chair. I put my own arm round her.

'Speak away,' I said. 'You are in front of the most impartial jury in the world.'

'Including you?'

'I'm not really in on this act.'

'As a fellow Scot,' said Laura, laying aside the *sgian dubh* with as much reluctance as Julius Caesar, according to Casca, laid aside the circlet which would have made him emperor of Rome, 'I can assure you we have nothing up our sleeve. All we are doing is to clear the ground. It's like one of those silly mathematics games, when, after the endless mental toil, you come back to the number you first thought of, so not to worry. We're only cutting away the dead wood.'

'James talks too much, but about what?' I asked, tightening the arm I had put round her. 'Look, Jane, nobody thinks James killed Carbridge, so what has he got to be so careful about?'

'He had a quarrel with Carbridge while we were on the tour.'

'Well, so had I,' I said. 'Fortunately for me, I can prove an alibi at the time of the murder. Can't James?'

'No, and I can't help him, but it's not as though you and he were the only ones. As a matter of fact, before we got to Fort William I think everybody was tired of Carbridge. He and Todd did the last part of the tour on their own, as I suppose you know. He had got under everybody's skin by that time. He used to call those office girls Red Sails in the Sunset. They laughed about it at first, but it got very tiresome when he laboured it. Then he called me Young Plover's Egg and when my feet began to play me up he tried to be funny about it — '

'*Did* he!' I said. 'I wish I'd heard him!'

'Then, the first time he called out "Toro! Toro!" when Todd came into the youth hostel common-room, Todd turned so white that I was afraid he was going to faint. Of course Carbridge saw he had upset him, so he harped on it. Then he used to call Perth the Old Woman Who Lived in a Shoe. It was difficult to deal with him because, on the surface, it was all so good-humoured and he never exactly insulted anybody.'

'Old boy, old boy!' I said savagely. 'What about Patsy Carlow and Coral Platt?'

'Oh, they took everything in good part and so did Freddie Brown. The other person who objected strongly to Carbridge was Lucius Trickett, but he contented himself by referring to half-baked oafs and he had as little to do with Carbridge as possible.'

'Most interesting,' said Dame Beatrice. Something in her tone told me that she had learned a fact which she badly needed to know. Vaguely I connected it with Sally Lestrange and poor old Bull's autobiography, although what brought that into my mind I could not say. Perhaps I really do have extra-sensory perception. Who knows? Anyway, Dame Beatrice rose from her chair with the satisfied smile of a snake which has tucked its goat safely into its gullet and is now prepared to sleep away the long process of digestion.

'Mr Carbridge certainly seems to have possessed the gentle art of making enemies,' she said.

Jane agreed and added, 'But without the slightest idea that *that* was what he was doing. He was the most myopic fool I ever met.'

'And, according to Perth, the onlooker who saw most of the game, he died *because* he was a fool,' I said.

Meanwhile, the police, pursuing their usual unspectacular, mundane, pedestrian tactics, had found what they were convinced was the murder weapon. Bingley, it seemed, had argued that the murderer would have had very little time to get rid of it, so that the chances were he had hidden it somewhere near at hand. The puzzle was to decide his reason for having substituted another knife for it.

'A case of muddled thinking,' Trickett said to me when we were discussing the case much later. 'He must have hoped to throw suspicion on Freddie and Coral and had no idea that the pathologist would spot it was the wrong knife.'

They looked in the obvious places at the hall of residence, such as under a loose floorboard they found in Trickett's study-bedroom when he pointed it out to them, and at the bottom of the lavatory cisterns and the big tank in the roof, and then one of the coppers noticed that the flowerbeds in the little garden which formed the centre of the London square in which the hall of residence was set had been freshly dug over, so they did a bit of digging on their own account and found what the pathologist agreed could be the knife which had administered to the choked and dying Carbridge his *coup de grâce*.

It was not difficult to establish ownership. Called upon separately, Trickett, Freddie, Coral, Patsy, Perth, Tansy and Rhoda identified the dagger as the antique which had been given to Todd. Todd made no attempt at a denial, but said merely (and calmly) that he recognised the knife, that he had lost it soon after his return home and that he could offer no explanation of how it had got into the flowerbed. The police pointed out that it had also got into Carbridge's body.

'How did you get on with him?' they asked. 'Did you like him?'

'*Like* the fellow?' he said. 'With everybody else I got heartily sick of him by the time that Scottish walk was over, but there was no harm in him. In fact, I had more to do with him than with anybody else on the tour and we finished at Fort William as a twosome, everybody else having chickened out and gone by bus. Any reason to murder the chap? Good Lord, if we were all murdered for our nuisance-value, who would be alive today? Not my Inspector of Taxes, to name but one!'

# 17

## *A Motive for Murder*

Hera and I had attended Carbridge's funeral. So had the warden and his wife, the Scottish tour party and one or two of the students who had made up the orchestra, but of friends and relatives there was no sign. I remembered that none of his own kind had come forward to identify the body and, although I had never liked the chap, I found myself feeling very sorry for him. I began to understand his compulsive gregariousness. He was dependent on strangers for all his social contacts. In other words, nobody had ever really loved him. I stood back mentally and looked at myself. I did not like to think that we were two of a kind.

After all the revelations about Carbridge's unpopularity, I said as much to Elsa. At the time I was feeling reasonably well pleased, for I had met and vanquished our Luella Granville Waterman. 'She was clay in my hands,' I said.

'Well, you owe that to me,' said Elsa. 'When she turned up and asked whether you had recovered sufficiently to talk to her, I said that only your conscientious devotion to our authors had brought you back into harness and I warned her that, if you were excited or frustrated in any way, the chances were that you would drop dead at her feet. We need to keep the old stagers like her, Comrie. They may not be bestsellers, but they're steady and, like Tennyson's brook, they go on forever.'

I said I felt sorry for the old girl and would always do my best for her and it was then that I added my reflections concerning Carbridge and myself.

'Don't waste your sympathy on *him*,' said Elsa. 'People who have no friends don't deserve to have any. You couldn't stand the man, if you remember, and you don't seem to have been the only one.'

'Well, he irritated me, I allow, but I stopped short of murdering him, anyway.'

'His will has finally been proved,' she said. 'He left quite a lot of money, and all of it to Todd.'

'Good Lord! But that's a motive for murder, if ever there was one! Money is nearly always at the bottom of these things.'

'Todd may not have known the contents of the will until it was proved. He is entitled to the benefit of the doubt.'

'What do you mean by "quite a lot of money"? Hundreds? Thousands?'

'About twenty thousand. It seems a lot of money to a poor soul like me.'

'It wouldn't even buy half a house.'

'Oh, don't be silly, Comrie. Nobody buys a house outright. What are mortgages for?'

'They equate with the millstones people hang round their own or other people's necks. So Carbridge left his money to Todd. That much of what you say must be true because you know I can check on it. If he left Todd his money, it would be because he liked the chap, although I must say he used to rile him with his teasing. Young Jane Minch made that very clear.'

'I expect he showed off in front of other people and hoped to raise a laugh at Todd's expense, but, from what you've told Sandy and me from time to time, weren't the two of them really very thick? Weren't they walking on their own quite a bit when you were walking The Way?'

'I wouldn't say "quite a bit", but I think they pushed on ahead of the students and the Minches when the students and Perth loitered to chip bits off the rocks and Jane's feet got so sore. I carried her back to the hostel on one occasion, I remember.'

Elsa grinned.

'The devil you did!' she said. 'What on earth did Hera say to that? And was it really necessary?'

'To your first question the answer is self-evident. Hera was not very pleased. As to whether it was necessary to transport the girl in the manner indicated, let's just say that I wanted the wench in my arms, but don't ask me why.'

'Was it satisfactory?'

'Yes, it was.'

'I had better begin pricing-up fish-slices, or would you rather have a tea-strainer?'

Dame Beatrice telephoned me on the following day to ask me to accompany her on a visit to the warden at the hall of residence. He had terminated his vacation and was staying there be-because he had plenty to do before the new term began. I could not imagine what more Dame Beatrice required of the warden, still less could I fathom her purpose in taking me with her to visit him. When I told Sandy I had to be out of the office again, all he said was, 'And to think I once fondly imagined that you worked here!' I said I had an idea that we were about to reach a climax in the matter of finding out who had killed Carbridge but, when Dame Beatrice and I reached the hall of residence next day, her first question to the warden gave no hint of this.

'Would you mind telling me how long you have been in charge here?' she asked.

'I have been here for a little more than five years. My predecessor retired at the end of an Easter term and I took over in the following May.'

'Had you any previous knowledge of any of the students who were here when you took office?'

'No, none of them, nor would they have known me. I came here from Hull, and at the time I had no contacts in London.'

'Would there be records of former residents of this hall? — students, I mean.'

'Oh, yes, of course. We like to keep up with our students' future progress. Some of them turn out to be quite notable people in their own field.'

'I imagine you do not keep records of those attendant on them while they are in residence.'

'If you refer to the cook and the maids and so forth, no, we do not. I inherited the domestic staff when I accepted the post

and they have remained faithful, I am glad to say. I suppose
your immediate interest is in the man Bull. He, too, was here
when I came and, on the whole, has given very satisfactory
service.'

'Would it be possible for me to look at your lists of former
students?'

'Of course, Dame Beatrice. As a matter of fact, I myself
looked them over not long after that unfortunate party to see
if I recognised the names of any of the older guests, as it seemed
likely that whoever committed the murder had an inside knowledge of the building. I was very much in two minds whether to
grant permission to Trickett to hold that party. Parties can be
allowed, and *are* allowed, during term, but then, of course, my
wife and I are on hand and can keep a grasp on the reins.
However, Trickett is a steady, reliable youth, so I acceded to his
request. How much I wish I had not!'

'Few of us have the gift of foresight,' said Dame Beatrice. 'I
am particularly interested in the name Todd.'

'The strange thing is,' the warden said, 'that the only Todd I
could find would be at least sixty-five years of age by now. It is
really rather puzzling.'

'And most intriguing,' said Dame Beatrice, 'because the Todd
I have in mind must have changed his name.' The warden produced his lists. As Dame Beatrice finished checking each year's
intake, she handed the document to me. It appeared that the
hall of residence could accommodate thirty-six students in
groups of twelve, for as the normal college course lasted for
three years, twelve students were all that could be admitted in
any particular year. I took the precaution of going back twenty-
five years, but the only Todd that I, like the warden, tracked
down, was indeed an elderly gentleman who could not possibly
be the Todd we were after.

We worked steadily through the lists and then Dame Beatrice,
handing them back, remarked, 'You appear to get a number of
foreign students here.'

'Most places of higher education do. Here we get West
Indians, Pakistanis, students from other parts of India, occa-

sionally one or two from European countries – '

'And, if his name is anything to go by, one from Spain.'

'Spain?' said the warden. Dame Beatrice handed him one of the documents. 'Oh, yes, a man named Grantoro. Why did you single out that name? Simply because it is Spanish?'

'I have never met it before.' Both the warden and I saw this as an evasive answer and Dame Beatrice realised this and cackled. ' "The proper study of mankind is man",' she said, 'and the study of man includes the language he uses to disguise (we are told) his thoughts.'

I glanced at her and light dawned on me.

'*Toro*,' I said, 'means bull. *Grantoro*, big bull.'

'Exactly,' said Dame Beatrice. 'I wonder, Mr Terrance, whether we might send for your caretaker?'

Puzzled but acquiescent, the warden touched the bell and sent a servant to find Bull. As soon as the old man saw Dame Beatrice, he stiffened and a look of obstinacy came into his face, but it was to me he spoke. 'I've give it up,' he said. 'The young lady don't want to do me life story. She ain't been nowhere near me all this week.'

'No. She is away from home,' said Dame Beatrice. 'Bull, why did you tell her (and Mr Melrose here) all those lies about your former profession?'

'They wasn't lies. I *was* assistant to the public executioner.'

'Yes, in a Spanish province, not in England. You were not a hangman, but a garrotter. Your son was so bitterly ashamed of your public image that he did not register at the polytechnic in your name, but translated it to Grantoro.'

'That wasn't nothing to do with my job. I'd give it up. It was because he didn't care to be known as the caretaker's son.'

'Why didn't you admit you knew Carbridge?' asked the warden. 'You recognised the body as soon as you saw it, didn't you? Carbridge and your son were fellow students here, although Grantoro was a third-year and Carbridge a first-year. This morning, I received a letter from my predecessor, who has only just heard about the murder. He says that, several years ago, Carbridge also changed his name. He is down in the lists simply as "Bridge" — that's why no one noticed before.'

'And at some time during their student days,' said Dame Beatrice, 'Bridge found out that Todd, then calling himself Grantoro, was your son and he also found out what your former profession had been. My granddaughter found that out, too, and decided that she wanted no more to do with your auto-biography. Mere squeamishness, of course, but most girls are squeamish when it comes to putting an iron collar round a criminal's neck and tightening it until it throttles him. A drop at the end of a rope seems infinitely preferable to women if a criminal has to be executed.'

Bull said sullenly that the men he had dealt with were mur-derers, and that they deserved what they got. He added that he had always wanted to have his son educated in England.

'I wanted as he should better himself,' he said. 'I wanted as he should have chances I did not have. I was twenty-four years of age when the Spanish Civil War started. I was married to an English girl and we had the one kid. She, the wife, didn't like my job, either, so, what with the war and everything, I quit and we all come back here to live. I never let on what my job had been, thinking it would go against me, but I got work and built meself up a character for being reliable, which, as Mr Terrance will testify, I am, and when the job here was going they give it to me and I been here ever since, which I hope, if there's going to be trouble, as Mr Terrance, sir, you will bear witness as I have always give satisfaction.'

The warden may or may not have intended to answer this appeal, but just then the telephone rang. Bingley was on the line.

'I'll take it in my study,' said the warden. He left us and we were aware of a seriously alarmed Bull.

'What's *he* want with the warden?' he asked in anxious tones.

'Perhaps we shall know when the warden comes back,' said Dame Beatrice. 'Was it your idea or did my granddaughter her-self decide not to attempt your autobiography?'

'Reckon you knows the answer to that as well as I does, or better.'

'I think your life was threatened if you published. As for Sally, I thought she might be in some danger, too, so I took steps to remove her from your orbit.'

'I wouldn't have harmed a hair of her head. We didn't reckon we had enough of me memoirs to make into a book, that's all.'

The warden was gone for what seemed a very long time. Bull became restless and, it was obvious, more and more uneasy.

'I better be going,' he said.

'Not until the warden comes back,' said Dame Beatrice. Such was the force of her personality that Bull re-seated himself in the chair from which he had risen and, muttering something about 'suit yourself', he leaned back, closed his eyes and opened them again only when the warden, Bingley and Bingley's sergeant came in.

'Well, Bull,' said the detective-inspector, 'Dame Beatrice has told me an interesting little story. I should like to know what you think of it. Of course I could tell it to you down at the station, but I daresay the warden and Mr Melrose would like to hear it, so I'll tell it here and now. It concerns an honest man and a devoted father.'

'You got nothing on me or on my boy.'

'In other words, you don't want to hear my story. Well, I don't blame you. But why on earth, man, when you found the body in the loo passage, did you substitute another knife for the one you found in the wound? And I can tell you, before you answer me, that you may think yourself lucky that, owing to Dame Beatrice's good offices on your behalf, I am not going to hold you as an accessory after the fact of murder. I ought to, but, as she points out, there are extenuating circumstances attaching to this case.'

'I suppose,' said Dame Beatrice, addressing Bull, 'you thought you were helping your son by trying to throw suspicion on those two young people who were preparing the food for the party.'

'I swear I never thought of nothink of that sort. All I wanted was to — was to — I don't know how to put it.'

'Create a diversion? Provide a red herring?'

'Sommat o' that sort, I s'pose, but, honest, I never knowed as the knife belonged to the young lady student. I thought as how it were one of our own cook's knives and I knowed she couldn't be blamed, being on 'er 'olidays at the time and the rest o' the kitchen staff likewise. There was plenty of other students millin' around. I didn't think the police would be able to pin the knife on anyone special, honest I never!'

'I suppose it was you who buried the dagger we found in the garden in the square,' said Bingley. 'I really ought to run you in. You had a key to that garden — '

'Who says I has?'

' — and, of course, you found the body long before Mr Melrose stumbled upon it. That is when you removed the electric lightbulb by standing on a kitchen chair. You recognised the antique knife as the one your son had shown you, the present he was given by a woman member of the tour party.'

'I still don't know what you're b— well talking about. Look, I got to make a phone call, so you'll 'ave to excuse me.'

'The only phone call you're going to make is to your lawyer, if you've got one,' said Bingley, 'and then I'm going to lock you up for a couple of days. I don't want Todd skipping because you've warned him. I suppose he didn't have time to remove that knife from the body before he was disturbed.'

It was not Bull, but I, who made a telephone call. It was to Hera. I asked whether Todd was with her. She replied that he was not and that she was not expecting him.

'To settle a bet,' I said, 'did you marry Todd or a man called Grantoro?'

'You had better come round,' she said. When I got there, I thought she looked ill. I asked whether she was all right. She said that she had been seeing her lawyer. 'A divorce has been arranged and will shortly take place,' she said with a little smile.

'You're ditching Todd? I'm glad to hear it,' I said, but I did not tell her why.

'I'm ditching Todd,' she said.

'Did you ever know him as Grantoro?'

'Yes, just at first, but I said I wasn't going to sign myself Hera

Grantoro. It sounds like one of those frightful names third-rate actresses take, thinking it will look good to theatrical agents and on the programme, if ever it gets that far.'

'You appear to have a peculiar phobia about names. I can remember when you didn't want to be known as Mrs Comrie Melrose.'

'Am I being given another chance to think that one over? Nothing doing, I'm afraid,' she said. 'What about you?'

'No,' I said. 'I think I'm settling for the babies who will look like plover's eggs.'

'Why have you come round here?'

'That doesn't matter now that you've settled for a divorce from Todd.'

She looked at me shrewdly and said, 'You came with the intention of telling me that, if I took on Todd again, I could look forward to a longer separation than the one he and I have had already. Well, as you say, it doesn't matter now.'

'I suppose,' said Elsa, 'it was Dame Beatrice who found out about the murder. How did she manage to pin it on Todd, not on Bull?'

'There were only three people concerned who knew how that dead convict had been murdered on Rannoch Moor. He was partially strangled and then, while I suppose he was too groggy to put up any resistance, the murderer stabbed him in the back. I read all the Scottish papers, thanks to Dame Beatrice and Laura Gavin. Carbridge was killed in just such a double-dose way. I had told Hera about it and I suppose at some time she told Todd. Somebody said that the hall of residence business was a copy-cat murder. Well, I knew that Hera and I were out of it because we were in one another's company for the whole of that Saturday afternoon.'

'I don't see how Dame Beatrice worked it all out,' said Sandy.

'Jane Minch gave her the real clue, I fancy, when she described how Carbridge used to rile people. To Todd he would shout "Toro! Toro!". I was present once when he did this. He even put two fingers to his forehead to represent horns and cavorted about, making bull-like rushes at everybody. I don't know why Todd didn't murder him on the tour.'

'They were alone together too much. He wouldn't have risked it,' said Elsa. 'He would have been the only suspect.'

'Yes. The party was the ideal place for the murder. Todd knew there would be several people there who had good reason to want Carbridge dead. Anyway, Dame Beatrice made a connection between Toro and Bull which doesn't seem to have occurred to anybody else, not even to the students who knew Bull as the caretaker at their hall of residence.'

'I suppose the one person of all others who had to be kept from the knowledge of what Bull's horrible profession had been was Hera,' said Elsa.

'I imagine so. I think she must have given Todd reason, while we were on the tour, to believe that she was willing to go back to him, and she is so fastidious that for the oafish Carbridge to let her know that Bull had been the judicial garrotter in a Spanish province would have put paid to Todd's chances. He dared not trust Carbridge's strange sense of humour. He has confessed everything now.'

'What about the knife? The newspaper report was that it had been found.'

'Yes, Bull had buried it. He found the body while Coral and Freddie were out to tea. The knife was still in it. I suppose Todd was too greatly agitated by what he had done to stop and pull the knife out. Bull recognised the knife because Todd had shown it to him in a pub where they used to meet occasionally when Bull was off duty.'

'Obviously the murder was premeditated, however much horror Todd felt when he had carried it out,' said Elsa.

'Yes. He made an arrangement to meet Carbridge on the afternoon of the students' party with a promise that they would work up a practical joke — just the sort of thing to appeal to Carbridge, I imagine. They both knew about the basement entrance, of course, and I expect Todd suggested they meet there so they could slip in without being seen. Anyway, Hera was right. It was *Sweeney* Todd after all.'

'What about you and Hera?' asked Elsa.

'All washed up, I'm afraid. The West Highland Way did its job,' I said. 'Todd's lawyers are going to plead extreme provocation and I hope they get away with it. There were times when, if I'd had the guts, I would have strangled Carbridge myself, and I don't believe I was the only one who felt like doing it.'

I went to see Hera before Todd's trial came on. She was calm and courageous. I did not know what to say to her, but she helped me out.

'Don't worry,' she said. 'I should never really have taken up with him again. I knew I didn't want to and that was long before I knew what he had done to that wretched Carbridge. What an oaf and what a fool that man was! If anybody ever deserved to be murdered, it's that kind of insensitive buffoon.'

'Have you — well, have you made any plans for the future?' I asked awkwardly.

'No, but I shall be all right. I shan't bother to divorce Barney because I know now that I shall never marry again, so there's no point in freeing myself. I shall stick to my maiden name of Camden, of course. After all, it's the name I've always used in my work.'

I looked at her. She held out both hands to me and I took her in my arms and kissed her for the last time. For us, as Philip Larkin, in a different context, has said, 'this frail travelling coincidence' was over.